Fairy Tales and Fables from Weimar Days

Fairy Tales and Fables from Weimar Days

Edited and Translated by Jack Zipes

The University of Wisconsin Press

The University of Wisconsin Press
114 North Murray Street
Madison, Wisconsin 53715

3 Henrietta Street
London WC2E 8LU, England

Fairy Tales and Fables from Weimar Days was first
published in 1989 by University Press of New England.
The University of Wisconsin Press reprint was first
published in 1997.

Library of Congress Cataloging-in-Publication Data
Fairy tales and fables from Weimar days / edited and translated by
   Jack Zipes.
      222 pp.   cm.
      Translated from German.
      Includes bibliographical references and index.
      Summary: A collection of literary fairy tales written during the
   Weimar Republic in Germany, intended to serve as utopian tales for
   raising the political consciousness of the young people of that
   period. Includes a scholarly introduction giving the social and
   cultural background of the tales.
      ISBN 0-299-15744-X (pbk.: alk. paper)
      1. Fairy tales—Germany. 2. Children's stories, German—
   Translations into English. [1. Fairy tales. 2. Short stories.]
   I. Zipes, Jack David.
   PZ8.F168599   1997
   [Fic]—dc21   97-10795

For David Bathrick
Who Has Kept the Weimar Spirit Alive

Contents

Kings, Tyrants, Misers, and Other Fools

Animal Wisdom

Freedom through Solidarity

Introduction

Recovering the Utopian Spirit of the Weimar Fairy Tales and Fables

hy, all of a sudden, so it seems, did highly political men and women, completely committed to furthering class struggle in Germany during the Weimar period, begin in 1920 to write and illustrate fairy tales and fables for children? What was it that impelled gifted political writers to dedicate themselves to transforming traditional fairy tales and fables into remarkable utopian narratives and provocative social commentaries until the Weimar Republic's collapse in 1933? There are no simple answers to these questions because many of the writers of the utopian tales disappeared, were killed by the Nazis, or were forced into exile, where they left few records about their work. Nevertheless, there are enough traces of their fairy-tale productivity during the Weimar period that we can regain an understanding of their efforts, which also means recovering their utopian spirit for the present.

The Weimar period (1919–1933) is perhaps one of the most critical epochs in German history, for it marked the first time that Germans tried democracy, and it also gave birth to national socialism. Nothing stood still during the Weimar Republic. It began with financial and political instability, thousands of homeless people, vast experimentation in the arts, and the reformation of public institutions. The Social Democrats endeavored to prevent the nation from falling apart at the seams and compromised its socialist policies from the beginning. From 1923 to 1929, it appeared that their politics of compromise might work. However, the worldwide economic depression of 1929 dashed the German experiment with democracy, and by 1933 the Nazis had brought about a revolution of German society that perverted the utopian dreams of all of those who had sought to revolutionize German society in 1918–1919 and had failed.

The Youth Movements

Paradoxically, the utopian fairy tales and fables were engendered by the failed revolutions of 1918–1919, for these stories reflected the mistakes made by German revolutionaries, and they also depicted the extent to which class conflicts remained unresolved. That is, once the radical Spartacus group, under the leadership of Rosa Luxemburg and Karl Liebknecht, and the workers/soldiers movement was defeated in Berlin and Hamburg by the end of 1918, once the Munich Räterepublik (soviet republic) was overthrown in the spring of 1919 and the Hungarian Räterepublik was vanquished in 1920, the Communists and other radicals were compelled to withdraw, analyze their mistakes, and set new policies and strategies to recommence their struggle for power in Germany.

Almost all political parties and groups realized after World War I that Germany's destiny would depend on the education and socialization of the young, and consequently the period between 1919 and 1933 saw the flowering of hundreds of youth groups, along with numerous endeavors to reform the public school system and the living and working conditions for children and teenagers. Of course, the origins of the youth movement can be traced back to the formation of the Wanderbund (1896), which led to the Wandervogel (Wandering Bird) movement in 1900, an uprising against the materialist values and decadence of the upper classes. However, the Wandervogel groups, which remained fairly active until the demise of the Weimar Republic, were geared to teenagers and university students of the middle classes. The emphasis was on a return to nature, comradeship, holistic living, and resistance against arbitrary authority. The groups tended to be exclusive and apolitical, so they were easily co-opted by the German regime to serve military interests during World War I; and even though the Wandervogel groups became more antiauthoritarian after the war, they never established a political program that addressed the majority of the young in Germany. Therefore, if anything, this movement provided a retreat from politics and an ideology concerned with the "purity" of life and nature that eventually benefited the Nazi cause.

In contrast to the Wandervogel movement, the three major political alignments that developed after World War I—the Social Democrats (SPD), the Communists (KPD), and the National Socialists (NDSAP)—focused a great deal of their energy on organizing the young from the working class and the lower middle class—in other words, the disenfranchised majority. The reasons these political parties took a great interest in the youth is clear: the dissatisfaction on the part of young people with the existing conditions in Germany had turned them into potential revolutionaries, and they had shown this in their participation in the November Revolution of 1918 and in their work in the Bavarian Räterepublik. During the early years of the Weimar Republic, from 1919 to 1924, thousands of youngsters were homeless; if they did have a home, it was often a room inhabited by several people. Prostitution and crime among the working classes became a "normal" way to earn a living. The school system neglected the needs of working-class and lower-class children and was geared to send those children out to work by the time they were twelve, whereas middle-class children were channeled through schools that led to the university. Moreover, the school system was run in a bureaucratic and authoritarian manner that permitted corporal punishment and provided little consultation with parents. There was virtually no sex education, and abortions were illegal. The majority of children and teenagers who found work were generally given meager wages and suffered under poor working conditions. Given the devastating inflation from 1919 to 1924 and the chaotic temper of the times, which often led to military conflict and violent strikes, growing up in Weimar Germany led to a feeling of tremendous instability and fear among the young.

To offset the miserable conditions and the disquietude of the German youth, the Social Democrats, the Communists, and the National Socialists formed extremely effective youth movements to mobilize the young, supposedly in the interests of the youth but basically to serve the interests of their respective parties. This is not to deny the fact that a vast number of adults were genuinely concerned about the plight of the young and sought to make their particular political parties or social organizations responsive to the problems faced by children and teenagers. Moreover, to the extent that the interests of the young and the political parties often coincided, it would be fair to say that the German youth felt in many instances that their needs were being addressed, or might be addressed, and they responded commensurately to the politics and programs of the parties as they saw fit.

In 1919 the SPD formed its youth group, called the Verband der Arbeiterjugendvereine Deutschlands, which changed its name in 1922 to the Verband der sozialistischen Arbeiterjugend (SAJ, the Union of Young Socialist Workers). At the time it had more than one hundred thousand members, mainly teenagers. In 1927 the Rote Falkengruppen (Red Falcon Groups) were organized as part of the SAJ movement. In addition, the SPD founded the Kinderfreunde (Friends of Children) movement that organized children between the ages of eight and twelve and published two important journals, *Der Kinderfreund* and *Kinderland.* The SPD's focus was not emphatically political, in contrast to the KPD and NSDAP. For instance, it did *not* seek to create major changes in the tracking system of the schools or in the basic hierarchical structure. The SPD focused on providing "neutral" cultural conditions in schools and other institutions to allow children of all social classes to develop a moral character and the virtues necessary for the creation of a genuine democratic society. Social change was thus dependent on the *evolution* (not revolution) of society based on human rights such as freedom of speech, religion, and thought. However, the SPD youth organizations outside school did try to provide a more critical "socialist" viewpoint and built youth centers in which important educational, artistic, and sport programs were developed for the young to provide them with meaningful leisure time. In this regard, the SPD did not endeavor to make political activists out of its members but sought to provide enlightenment on affairs that concerned them. Only toward the end of the Weimar Republic did the SPD youth organizations play a militant role in party politics. In general, the SPD's youth movement supported the liberal humanistic programs of the government without questioning some of the more debatable authoritarian and class-biased institutions geared toward educating the young.

It was just the opposite with the Communist party. In 1920 it formed the Freie Sozialistische Jugend (FSJ), which was transformed into the Kommunistische Jugend Deutschlands (KJD, the Communist Youth of Germany) and grew to more than fifty thousand members. The major focus of the Communists was to make political activists out of the young, and it was for this reason that their platform, even when it shifted somewhat over the years, always included a program to change the school system and the factories. Because the schools were established according to tracking systems that benefited the rich, the Communists fought for changes that would do away with such tracking and bring about a general education combining vocational, scientific, and humanistic programs specifically directed toward overcoming exploitation and hierarchies in the workplace and at home. Everything was to be oriented toward bringing about the "dictatorship of the proletariat," so the Communist local and cell groups structured their youth-center programs around activities that furthered a sense of class struggle. Of course, there were also sports and cultural programs that were not directly involved in the class struggle. However, for the most part, the young were indoctrinated into party politics and encouraged to develop political plays supporting the Communist program and to carry on agit-prop programs up through 1933.

In like manner, the National Socialists intended their youth organizations to be politically active and to reinforce their race and culture programs. In 1926 the Hitlerjugend (Hitler Youth) and the NS-Deutscherstudentenbund (the NS German Student League) were formed, and they copied the youth work that Communist and Socialist youth organizations had already been doing—obviously with a different emphasis. The National Socialists set up a comprehensive indoctrination program based on the *Führerprinzip;* it sought through the use of uniforms, symbols, and military discipline to provide a "nationalistic community" that would oppose the dangers of a Marxist conspiracy and/or a Jewish capitalist takeover. It is interesting to note that almost 40 percent of the NSDAP membership in 1931 was under thirty, for the National Socialists were able to channel the anger and frustration of the young into paramilitary action, with total belief in and obedience to a "messianic" figure like Hitler. The Nazis were not interested in transforming the school system but in taking it over and cleansing it of the "filth" that had bespoiled Germany. Moreover, they formed tight-knit units throughout Germany in which sports and cultural programs were intended to strengthen the resolve of a pure German youth for the great struggle to save Germany.

Given the grim situation of the majority of young people in Germany from 1919 to 1933 and the intense competition of the different political parties to win their support—and the other conservative and liberal parties had their youth organizations as well—we must ask again: why in heaven's name would the more radical youth groups, leaders, and writers want to focus on developing special fairy tales as a means of contributing to the class struggle?

The Status of the Fairy Tale

Though it might seem at first a strange notion to accept, the fairy tale has always played a vital role in German politics. The oral folktales told by the peasants over the past centuries have always had a political and utopian aspect, and the literary fairy tales, which originated for adults and children at the end of the eighteenth century, were highly political. For instance, the romantic writers, who wrote mainly for adults, used the fairy tale to comment on the philistinism of the German bourgeoisie and the perversion of the Enlightenment ideals. The fairy tales written for children were filled with Christian references and were intended to socialize children according to the norms of the Protestant ethic. Moreover, many of the tales for adults and children contained allusions to the Napoleonic Wars as well as nationalist messages.

Throughout the nineteenth century the literary fairy tale, bolstered by the popularity of the collections of the Brothers Grimm and Ludwig Bechstein, grew in public favor, and by the beginning of the twentieth century it had virtually become *the* German genre par excellence. Indeed, if one were to scan the names of the most famous German authors, from Goethe to Thomas Mann, one would find very few who had not written at least one fairy tale. Of course, most of these tales were for adults and are vastly different in their themes and styles. But they reflect how seriously Germans take the fairy tale and how significant it is in their education and socialization. By the 1870s the Bechstein and Grimm fairy tales—and others such as Robert Reinecke's and Hans Christian Andersen's works—had been introduced into the school system and had become standard reading material for children. The traditional Christmas play, presented in the public theaters throughout Germany since the 1850s, became the fairy-tale play *Peterchens Mondfahrt* (Little Peter's Trip to the Moon); and if that particular play was not produced, another fairy-tale drama would be performed—a tradition that has continued to the present day. All in all, if one were to consider that the oral folktale tradition was still strong in Germany and served as the source for many of the literary fairy tales, it is not difficult to see that the fairy tale had become the most popular genre and served to provide a sense of community. That is, the shared referential system of the symbols and motifs of a cultivated fairy-tale canon gave German readers, young and old, a means to identify themselves with important aspects of German culture.

Certainly, as far as young listeners and readers were concerned, the fairy tale came to be used in a conservative sense that had political overtones. The predominant use of such classical tales as those of Cinderella, Little Red Riding Hood, Sleeping Beauty, Rumpelstiltskin, the Frog King, Rapunzel, Snow White, and others reinforced the patriarchal order and gender specification in German upbringing. The male hero is the adventurer, the doer, and the rescuer, whereas the female protagonist is generally passive if not comatose. Moreover, the Grimm and Bechstein tales often conserve a medieval notion of "might makes right" along with typical "bourgeois myths" of industriousness, cleanliness, and truthfulness as holiness. Generally speaking, the victor at the end of the classical tale is someone who is unique, exceptional, rising above all others in the tale.

It was particularly this elitist feature, which admittedly has beneficial psychological aspects for young children needful of positive ego reinforcement, that became cultivated in the literary fairy tales for children during the first three decades of the twentieth century. The major trend in fairy-tale books, largely published for middle-class children, was toward "redemptive" tales, in which an exceptional protagonist had magical adventures and exhibited a brand of goodness and harmony that conformed to the standards and expectations of conservative German society. The works of Hans Dominik (*Technische Märchen,* 1903), Sophie Reinheimer (*Von Sonne, Regen, Schnee und Wind,* 1907; *Aus Tannerwalds Kinderstube,* 1909), and Waldemar Bonsels (*Die Biene Maja,* 1912) are characteristic of this type of fairy tale, which was developed in three different ways during the 1920s.

First, there were numerous didactic tales, especially those published in children's journals and annuals like *Auerbachs Kinder-Kalender, Hahns Kinder- und Märchen-Kalender,* and *Die Jugendlust,* which incorporated orthodox religious notions and furthered conventional social ideas in a seemingly innocent manner. Generally speaking, the fairy-tale garb was used to cloak an ideology that rationalized the use of power in authoritarian ways.

Second, there were numerous idyllic fairy tales that were intended to divert children from confronting social problems and issues and make it appear that "magical intervention" could easily resolve conflicts of any kind. These tales were often exotic and sought to transport the young reader to other worlds, as in Clara Hepner's *Der Meister und seine Schüler* (1922). Some of the tales were ornamental pastiches, such as Frida Schanz's *Schneewittchens Hochzeit* (1928) and Ina Seidel's *Das wunderbare Geißleinbuch* (1925), in which classical tales were playfully patched together in an amusing way as though the social fragments of children's stressful lives could easily be reassembled in like manner.

Third, there were interesting revisions of the folktale tradition by Hans Blunck (*Märchen von der Niederelbe*, 1923; *Kindermärchen*, 1933), Otto Stückrath (*Märchen aus der Heimat*, 1924), Gottwalt Weber, (*Neue Deutsche Märchen*, 1926), and Wilhelm Matthiessen (*Der Kauzenberg*, 1933). Here the superstitions and traditional figures of German folklore were employed to show the threats to the peace and order of German society communal life. However, the eerie characters are banished, quite often by an innocent, good-natured hero, an archetypal figure representative of the "good-hearted" German. There were also tales that dealt with peasant heroes who saved their families through hard work and dedication against outside forces threatening the harmony of German society.

Given the basically conservative if not illusionary nature of these fairy tales and the fact that the fairy tale played such a dominant role in the socialization of children, it is no wonder, then, that one of the first points on the cultural agenda for children, by both the Social Democrats and the Communists, was the fairy tale, that is, a revision of the fairy tale. To be sure, such politicization of the fairy tale from a socialist viewpoint was not new. There had been attempts made at the end of the nineteenth century and the beginning of the twentieth century by F. S. Liebisch (*Ein Märchentraum: Die Königin der Arbeit beim Feste der Zwerge im Erdschatzreiche*, 1870), Friedrich Gottlieb Schulze (*Der große Krach*, 1875), Lorenz Berg and Emil Roßbach (*König Mammon und die Freiheit*, 1878), and Robert Grötzsch (*Nauckes Luftreise und andere Wunderlichkeiten* (1908), but they remained ineffective because there was very little cultural work being done toward developing a socialist movement for youth. It took World War I and a revolt by the young that has often been likened to "patricide" for political parties to address the needs of German youth in a more generalized and concerned manner.

Raising Political Consciousness through the Fairy Tale

An indication of the great emphasis that the Social Democrats and Communists were going to place on the fairy tale in their endeavors to shape the perspectives of the young can be gleaned from Erwin Hoernle's essay entitled *Grundfragen proletarischer Erziehung* (Basic Questions of Proletarian Education, 1923):

In general we must learn how to tell stories again, those fantastic, artless stories as they were heard in the weaving rooms and the homes of craftsmen in the pre-capitalist period. The thoughts and feelings of the masses were reflected here in a most simple way and therefore in the clearest way. Capitalism with its destruction of the family and mechanization of the working people has annihilated this old "folk art." The proletariat will create new fairy tales in which workers' struggles, their lives, and their ideas are reflected and correspond to the degree which they demonstrate how they can continually become human, and how they can build up new educational societies in place of the old decrepit ones. It makes no sense to complain that we do not have suitable fairy tales for our children.

Professional writers will not produce them. Fairy tales do not originate at the desk. The real fairy tale originates in an unconscious and collective way in the course of long periods of time, and the work of the writer consists at the most in smoothing over and rounding out the material at hand. The new proletarian and industrial fairy tale will come as soon as the proletariat has created a place in which fairy tales are not read aloud but told, not repeated according to a text, but created in the process of telling.

Hoernle, who was the Communist party's head of political education and who had already published innovative tales in *Die Oculi-Fabeln* (1920), was somewhat idealistic because the success of his program depended on the success of the Communist party and other radical political organizations in bringing about social reform in the schools and families. Yet he was not alone in his idealism, and there was a concerted effort by progressive writers and publishers to "proletarianize" the fairy

13

tale, especially during the period from 1920 to 1925. For instance, two journals, *Der junge Genosse* and *Jahrbuch für Arbeiterkinder,* which contained stories, poems, articles, and games for proletarian children, were founded in 1922. Anthologies with political tales and stories, such as *Proletarischer Kindergarten* (1921) edited by Ernst Friedrich and *Pflug und Saat* (1923) edited by Arthur Wolf, began to appear. Most important were the two series produced by the Malik publishing house in Berlin, which was close to the Communist party, and the Verlag für proletarische Freidenker in Dresden and Leipzig, which represented a radical movement against organized religion. Under the direction of Werner Herzefelde, who employed such great artists as Georg Grosz to illustrate the books, Malik published a series entitled "Märchen der Armen" (Fairy Tales of the Poor), which included *Was Peterchens Freunde erzählen* (Hermynia zur Mühlen, 1920), *Ali, der Teppichweber* (Hermynia zur Mühlen, 1923), *Die Dollarmännchen* (Eugen Lewin-Dorsch, 1923), and *Silavus* (Maria Szucisch, 1923).

The leading person behind the Verlagsanstalt für proletarische Freidenker was Arthur Wolf, who was concerned in publishing books of artistic nature that were socialist and antireligious. He was responsible for producing the following collections of fairy tales: *Sternekund und Reinekund* (Jozsef Lengyel, 1923), *Die Träume des Zauberbuchs* (Maria Szucisch, 1923), and *Rote Märchen* (Béla Illès, 1924). It is interesting to note that many gifted writers of the Hungarian emigration, such as Szucisch, Illès, Lengyel, and Balázs, wrote fairy tales and knew each other. All of their tales were translated by Stefan Klein, who was Hermynia Zur Mühlen's lifelong companion, and it was Hermynia Zur Mühlen who influenced other German writers to produce radical fairy tales. These political and personal connections between the writers were significant because they brought about a sense of solidarity that continued throughout the Wei-

Hermynia Zur Mühlen, *Was Peterchens Freunde erzählen* (Berlin: Malik, 1921). Illustrator: Georg Grosz.
Cover art.

mar period. However, there was a shift in the general attitude toward the fairy tale by the communist and progressive movements after 1926 that caused experimentation to abate somewhat.

When it became clear that the school reform movement would not succeed and that the proletarian tales and fables would not replace the "bourgeois" or traditional folktales in the schools and libraries, the left-wing political parties began to focus more on oral storytelling within the children's and youth groups and to emphasize more realistic stories that depicted the actual living conditions of the working classes. The cultural movement entered a strong agit-prop phase in 1926 that lasted until the Nazi takeover in 1933. Not only were traveling agit-prop plays produced by youth groups associated with the SPD and the KPD but also large choral performances. Moreover, social workers and psychologists began to organize the youth to counter the deplorable living conditions in urban environments. One of the most notable projects was Wilhelm Reich's Sex-Pol organization (1930–1933) in Berlin, which tried to deal with sexual problems in working-class families that were caused by socioeconomic deprivation.

The shift toward realism in literature and agit-prop in cultural activities between 1926 and 1933 did not lead to the total abandonment of the utopian and political fairy tale. For instance, Oskar Maria Graf published his collection *Licht und Schatten* in 1927; Robert Grötzsch issued the third edition of *Muz, der Riese* in 1927; Rosa Meyer-Leviné translated *Lenin-Märchen* in 1929; and Hermynia Zur Mühlen published *Es war einmal . . . und es wird sein* in 1930 and *Schmiede der Zukunft* in 1933. However, it was clear that Hoernle's initial hopes for a political fairy tale commensurate with the times and interests of the working classes did not take root and no longer had the support of either the Communist party or the Social Democratic party, as it had in the early 1920s. Still, the early development of the proletarian fairy tale did lead to some interesting experiments that might have had far-reaching ramifications if the Nazis had not come to power in 1933. These were in the area of theater.

In 1929 Lisa Tetzner, who had become famous as a traveling storyteller, collector of folktales, and writer of fairy tales, collaborated with Béla Balázs in composing the play *Hans Urian geht nach Brod* in 1929. There had been many other political fairy-tale plays for children during the 1920s, but this drama was the culmination of all of the previous works and the extraordinary work done in the youth groups. It was based on the French writer Paul Vaillant-Couturier's novel for children entitled *Jean sans Pain* (1921), which had been translated into German in 1928.

Vaillant-Couturier's work concerns a young boy named Jean who runs away from the impoverished conditions in his home. His father died during World War I, and his mother, who had worked in an armaments factory, is dying from a disease that she contracted there. It is Christmas, and Jean enters the woods, where he encounters a talking rabbit, who has been delegated by the other animals of the forest to reveal the "truth" to humankind so that human beings will become good and free. To accomplish this purpose, the rabbit, whose ears are used as propellers, flies to a large city and shows Jean the terrible conditions in a factory that cause the workers to suffer. Afterward they visit a restaurant, where industrialists, generals, and clergymen enjoy a sumptuous feast at the expense of the workers. The rabbit explains to Jean how such vast discrepancies in the society come about. When they are detected in the restaurant, they must flee.

Balázs and Tetzner transposed the story to the Depression year of 1929. Their protagonist, Hans, who goes to purchase bread for his starving family, encounters a magic rabbit, who is also seeking food, and the two of them begin a journey around the world to learn why they do not have money to purchase bread. Again the magic ears of the rabbit serve as propellers, and along the way they form a friendship with a young Eskimo and an American, the son of a capitalist factory-owner, who want to help them. In America this unique group of youngsters from different social classes, nationalities, and races starts learning more about the actual conditions of production that workers must endure, and they encounter exploitation of workers, militarism, and racism. Forced to flee when the rabbit's life becomes endangered, they eventually make their way to the Soviet Union, where they learn how to share and work with others in solidarity. Eventually, Hans and the rabbit make their way back to Germany, resolved to bring about a change in the living and working conditions in their society.

Balázs and Tetzner's play was written at a time when the Stalinization of the Soviet Union was in an early phase, so the Soviet Union was still considered the homeland of true communism and thus served as a guiding beacon in the play. As a result, the German drama transforms the French novel, which is more of an expressionist and moral outcry, into a much more political statement of solidarity and hope. *Hans Urian geht nach Brod* was produced on November 13, 1929, in Berlin, and given the climate of the times, it was very successful. Tetzner then adapted the play and made it into a novel, which she published in 1929 and 1931. It too enjoyed a popular reception and was translated into several other languages, including English.

In many respects, *Hans Urian geht nach Brod,* both as play and novel, was the result of the collected efforts of writers from the beginning of the political fairy-tale movement in 1920, and it is important to reconsider the major changes in the genre that had come about since Hoernle issued his call for a *new* industrialized fairy tale. Two tendencies are apparent in the utopian fairy tales and fables by progressive writers from 1920 to 1933:

(1) old tales are told anew, and (2) proletarian fairy tales have provocative and utopian implications.

The old tales told anew are generally based on well-known folktales and fables that were transformed to correspond to changing sociopolitical conditions. The "newness" of the tales has more to do with content than with form. For example, Hoernle's "The Poodle and the Schnauzer," Felix Fechenbach's "The Triumph of the Wolves," and Béla Illés's "The Fairy Tale about the Bear, the Wolf and the Sly Fox" are close to the traditional folktale and fable, but the "new" lessons to be learned are based on parallels to be drawn with the hegemonic conditions in Europe following World War I. Maria Szucisch's fairy-tale collection *Silavus,* which exposes the nature of autocratic rule, and Béla Balázs's "The Victor," which concerns the self-destructive nature of the military personality, draw on the oriental folktale tradition. The narrative style is not new, and to a certain extent, even the messages of these tales are not entirely specific to Weimar Germany. Yet this factor makes the tales appealing on a universal level, and they suggest certain "verities" of politics that will remain truthful as long as the social conditions that produce them remain the same. In this respect, though writers like Hoernle, Fechenbach, Szucisch, and Balázs did not invent new narrative strategies, they provoke their readers by demonstrating how certain political truths will continue to cause enslavement and suffering if the conditions that give rise to the truths are allowed to remain as they are. Their tales are thus more unsettling and provocative than hopeful insofar as they focus on the consequences of irresolute action and feeblemindedness.

Even more provocative, however, were the tales by Kurt Schwitters, and Joachim Ringelnatz, who did a great deal of experimentation by parodying traditional folktales in keeping with expressionism and dadaism. Schwitters's "Happiness" and Ringelnatz's "Kuttel Daddeldu Tells His Children the Story about Little Red Cap" satirize the traditional happy ending and quest for wealth, and in other tales (not included in this volume) they also experimented with nonsense, optical illusion, and montage. The parody of the folktale from a political perspective was developed more by writers for adults. Bertolt Brecht, Franz Hessel, Ödön von Horváth, Georg Kaiser, Mynona, and numerous other expressionist writers wrote tongue-in-cheek versions about the illusions created by fairy tales of how easily aspirations of success could be fulfilled. Because writers of fairy tales for children wanted to provide more hope for their audience, they shied away from such irony and tended to be more serious and straightforward.

The proletarian fairy tales were intended to compel young readers to think about their impoverished living conditions and the potential they had to change them through political action. That is, they were innovative exercises in raising political consciousness, and the style and content of the tales differed greatly, although there was a common denominator: the principle of hope. The purpose of all of the writers was to instill a sense of hope that a new, more egalitarian society could be realized if people recognized who the true enemy was—namely, capitalism in various disguised forms—and learned to work together to defeat that enemy. The major tendencies of these tales was to (1) project an ideal societal organization that would bring an end to all suffering, (2) portray children whose honesty and clairvoyance endowed them with the ability to expose hypocrisy and made them into harbingers of a bright future, (3) develop exemplary heroes who bring about solidarity and collaboration in a struggle against exploitation, (4) reveal how social class exploitation worked and how it could be stopped, and (5) show the brutality of war and competition and underline the need for peace and coexistence.

Almost all of these tendencies can be found in the

tales of Hermynia Zur Mühlen. By far the most productive, if not also the most creative, of the political fairy-tale writers, she was particularly concerned about inducing her readers to realize how they were manipulated by the rich and how they themselves contributed to their own exploitation by ignoring the devious ways of power-hungry people. The gullibility of the working people is the theme of "The Fence," "The Servant," and "The Glasses"; and Zur Mühlen demonstrates that the future emancipation of the proletariat will depend on the insights of the young who learn what solidarity means. The issue of sight and perspective is also apparent in Berta Lask's "The Boy Who Wanted to Fight with a Dragon," Carl Ewald's "A Fairy Tale about God and Kings," Maria Szucisch's "The Holy Wetness," Eugen Lewin-Dorsch's "The Wise Man," Heinrich Schulz's "The Castle with the Three Windows," and Anna Mosegaard's "The Spider." Lask focuses on the learning process a young boy must go through in order to grasp who the real dragons in the world are, and Ewald makes certain that his readers learn just who the people are who create kings. In fact, he has God himself put things into their proper perspective for human beings. Szuchsich, on the other hand, reveals how incapable God is when it comes to rectifying injustices on earth. Her ironic style is similar to that of Lewin-Dorsch, Schulz, and Mosegaard, who portray egotistical and greedy protagonists blind to the reality of their own existence. Such blindness, the authors reveal, will ultimately lead to the self-destruction of these men.

Though many of the tales deal with the grim situation of common people and their apparent helplessness, they are founded on the principle of hope, for both the disturbing and the utopian components of these tales *provoke* their protagonists and readers, simultaneously, to realize that something has to be done to change their situation. The prescriptions for curing the pauperization of the common people and for establishing a "classless"

Hermynia Zur Mühlen, *Was Peterchens Freunde erzählen* (Berlin: Malik, 1921). Illustrator: Georg Grosz. Cover art.

society are not written down. It is up to the reader to provide the closure to these tales, although there are other proletarian tales in which an end to suffering announces the beginning of a new, more egalitarian, if not socialist, society. All of Robert Grötzsch's tales, "The Enchanted King," "Burufu the Magician," and "Felix the Fish," describe the tenacity of little people to survive and withstand the forces of oppression. Like Grötzsch, Oskar Maria Graf demonstrates in "Baberlababb" and "The Fairy Tale about the King" how cruel tyrants will bring about their own downfall. Only when a despotic figure realizes how unjust he has been, like the junk dealer in Bruno Schönlank's "The Patched Pants," can there be redemption. Otherwise, the oppressed little people triumph in the end. The magical helpers in the tales represent the power of hope, the wish fulfillment necessary to keep the people and the readers hopeful that a just society can one day be established here on this earth.

The Demise and Rise of the Utopian Fairy Tales and Fables

Despite the philosophical elements of hope and the fine artistic quality of the utopian fairy tales and fables, they never took firm root in the public realm. The reasons for this "failure," if one can use such a term, are numerous: (1) the audience addressed by these tales was economically poor and for the most part could not afford to purchase the books and support the counter-cultural endeavor; (2) schools and libraries resisted these tales, and they did not gain entrance into the dominant distribution process necessary for any new type of literature to survive; (3) after 1926, the political experimentation with fairy tales and fables was not enthusiastically backed by the youth organizations of the SPD and KPD; (4) the major reading audiences, young and old, were reluctant to have their traditional fairy tales, such as those by Grimm, Hauff, Bechstein, and Andersen, replaced, and they tended to support the new "bourgeois" fairy tales, which were imitative of the Grimms' tales and did not challenge the status quo. In fact, if anything, reading audiences were swayed more and more to consume nationalist and *völkisch* tales in keeping with the growing chauvinism during the 1920s. One need only read the conservative and liberal magazines and annuals for children to note the increase in allusions and connections between traditional folk symbols and Nazi ideology. Typical of the general trend in Germany by 1934 is the following poem by Adolf Holst, who was one of the best-known poets and writers for children. He published this verse in *Auerbachs Kinder-Kalendar,* one of the leading journals for children at that time.

Der Drachentöter
Aus alten Mären, da klingt es
Von einem Dornröselein schön,
Von höllischem Zauber singt es,
Und seltsame Kunde bringt es
Von Hexen und Spindeldrehen.

Und wie ein König gekommen,
hundert Jahre danach,
Der hat die Feste erklommen
und dem Fluche die Macht genommen,
Der kûßte Dornröschen wach!

Es ist ein Ritter geritten
Durch schlafende deutsch Land,
Der hat mit der Hölle gestritten
Und der Brut des Drachens mitten
den Flamberg ins Herze gerannt!

Der Ritter sonder Fehle,
Da ward ihm das Wunder zuteil,
Und er hob aus der Dornenhöhle
Die herrliche deutsche Seele—
Und alles Volk schrie: "Heil!"

The Dragonslayer

The old tales ring forth about a sleeping beauty. They sing about a satanic power and bring reports about witches and spindles.

They tell how a king came one hundred years later. He climbed the walls and took the power away from the curse by kissing Sleeping Beauty awake!

A knight came a-riding through sleeping Germany. He fought with hell and ran through the dragon's heart in the middle of the flaming mountain!

The knight of a special errand was endowed with wondrous power, and he lifted the glorious German soul out of the cave of thorns. And all of the people cried out: "Heil!"

This poem was an omen of what was to come during the Nazi period. All progressive experimentation with fairy tales and folktales was banned. The tales by the Grimms, Hauff, Bechstein, and Andersen were appropriated by the Nazis and used and interpreted in accordance with national-socialist ideology. Those authors who wrote "new" literary fairy tales either shied away from politics and social problems in their tales or wrote tales with archaic folk elements that glorified Germans as a special race. The entire field of children's literature underwent a fascist transformation, and the utopian tendency of the fairy tale was perverted to glorify Hitler and the Third Reich.

After 1945 the association of fairy tales in general and the Grimms' fairy tales in particular with the Third Reich was so strong that the Allied occupation forces banned those tales during a brief period for contributing to the barbarity of the Nazis. Consequently, for a long time after World War II, there was little production or experimentation with fairy tales. Only gradually were the old classics reproduced, and if new tales appeared, they tended to be idyllic and somewhat puerile works that included stock fairy-tale characters in some predictable adventure that led to a happy end. Gone were the fascist renditions. Gone were the proletarian tales of the 1920s.

By 1968, however, with "revolution" in the winds of the German student and antiwar movements, there was

Eugen Lewin-Dorsch, *Die Dollarmännchen* (Berlin: Malik Verlag, 1923). Illustrator: Heinrich M. Davringhausen. Title Page.

a renascence of interest in the Weimar period. The anti-authoritarian students looked back in history for models to follow and were drawn to the experiments and politics of the Weimar Republic. By 1970 there were various reproductions of Zur Mühlen's tales and Hoernle's works. In particular, the interest in radical fairy tales was linked to the student movement's rediscovery of works by progressive educators and psychologists such as Siegfried Bernfeld, Alfred Adler, Wilhelm Reich, Otto Kanitz, and others and also to Walter Benjamin's writings about a proletarian children's theater. Moreover, the antiauthoritarian phase of the student movement prepared the way for a period when reform day-care centers were established, when schools and universities underwent a major democratic transformation, and when the general reading public became open to progressive ideas in the realm of children's culture. Ironically, the desired impact that the writers of the Weimar fairy tales and fables sought in the 1920s began having a powerful effect in the 1970s.

The result was great political and aesthetic experimentation with the fairy tale for children and young readers. In 1972–1973 alone, four books were produced that were to bring about a radical change in the future development of the literary fairy tale for children in West Germany: Christine Nöstlinger's *Wir pfeifen auf den Gurkenkönig,* Friedrich Karl Waechter's *Tischlein deck dich und Knüppel aus dem Sack,* Janosch's *Janosch erzählt Grimm's Märchen,* and Michael Ende's *Momo.* All four carried the imprint of the antiauthoritarian student movement and continued the heritage of the Weimar proletarian fairy tales in such a unique and compelling way that they had a huge success in West Germany. What's more, even though experimentation with the utopian fairy tale has abated somewhat, it has not really stopped; and by and large, the experimental fairy tale for children, with utopian elements that originated in the days of the Weimar Republic, continues to serve as the model for the best among the German writers of fairy tales.

It has taken well over sixty years for the Weimar tales to come into their own. But it is not a coincidence that this has happened, for they still speak to us today with urgent voices. The questions they ask and the issues they raise have not been resolved, and we are still confronted with exploitation, ecological disaster, class struggle, war, racism, and hypocrisy. Recovering the utopian spirit of these Weimar tales can thus serve as a reminder that their narratives of hope are still awaiting fulfillment and that ultimately we, and no divine power, are responsible for making this world a better place for future generations.

Learning from Mistakes

Kurt Schwitters

Happiness

(1925)

nce upon a time there were three sisters who looked alike. They weren't beautiful. They weren't rich. They weren't smart. But they lived simply, quietly, and contentedly. Then the three had different dreams. The first one dreamed that great happiness would be bestowed upon them. The second dreamed that they would be able to find happiness by themselves with the help of a gypsy. The third dreamed that they would find happiness only if they made the right wish. And then a gypsy happened to arrive soon after the dreams. She had a bundle of presents under her arm and gave each sister a choice. The first sister wished to be beautiful; the second, to be rich; the third, to be smart. Then the gypsy said, "Your wishes are bad," and she disappeared.

The first sister became so beautiful that the sun did not dare to shine because the young woman was more beautiful than the precious sun itself. Whenever she went out, she was immediately followed by a hundred men because she was so beautiful. And if another woman encountered her, that woman would curse her and turn away because she was so beautiful. The married men loved her more than their own wives because she was so beautiful, and their wives wanted to scratch out her beautiful eyes because they were so beautiful. The men dueled in her behalf and shot each other because she was so beautiful. And she only stood there and laughed; she could do nothing else but laugh because she was so beautiful. But the more beautiful she became, the more she became sick since death has no fear of beauty. And when she was about to die, all of the men cried with broken hearts because she was so beautiful and all of the women rejoiced because she had to die. And the familiar gypsy appeared before her deathbed and said, "You should have wished for health!" Then the beautiful woman died.

The second sister became extremely rich. She lived outside the city in a villa in a gigantic park with lakes and artificial mountains. She had her own airport, numerous cars and sofas, and servants and friends, just as much as she wanted. That was how rich she was. And her ships sailed in the waters of India and Palestine and Australia and Greenland. That was how rich she was. And she spread butter lavishly on cheese and never ate bread or potatoes. That was how rich she was. And she had a husband who admittedly did not love her, but he did anything she wanted. That was how rich she was. And she had her own language and her own kind of phonetic script invented for her correspondence. That was how rich she was. And whenever she went to the theater in the evening, she bought out the entire house and sat completely alone in the former royal loge with her Pomeranian dogs, pearls, and diamonds. That was how rich she was. Once when she went walking and saw a child on the street with some buttered bread, she became vexed because the buttered bread did not belong to her as well. That was how rich she was. Then she met the gypsy again, who said to her, "Your wish was wrong, for you are not content. You should have wished for contentment. Then you could easily do without all of your riches."

The third sister had become smart. She was so smart that she knew the Bible in its original version by heart and could recite it backward and forward and could produce the cubic roots of twenty digital numbers from her head. She was so smart that she herself knew that she was not beautiful. She was so smart that she knew that men could not stand her because of her brains, for she could think much faster and much better than any man. That was how smart she was. Eternity was for her only a question of space and time, which could not be acquired with money, and she was so smart that she knew that being smart was entirely insignificant to feeling happy. Yes, she even knew that the opposite was true, that dumb people feel much happier than smart people. And she herself had also felt much better in the past than she did right at that moment. She knew just about everything. For instance, she knew that something would happen again in the Balkans, and she knew that peace conferences would only lead to the next war, and that pacifists were nothing more than strategic pawns for the Bolsheviks. She even knew where the gypsy lived, and she went there. She was so smart that she returned her present to her. Then the gypsy said, "You also made the wrong choice, but what would you like now instead?" The third sister replied, "Wisdom."

Then the gypsy said, "I don't have to give you that because you have it already."

So the third sister succeeded in becoming happy because she managed to free herself of human desires, and she knew that she had been happy before the gypsy had arrived and given her the fatal gift of smartness.

Carl Ewald

A Fairy Tale about God and Kings

(1921)

nce upon a time the people became so sick and tired of their kings that they decided to send some deputies to God to ask for his help against their monarchs.

The deputies arrived at the gates of heaven and were allowed to enter heaven in turn. But when the speaker of the group presented their case, God shook his head in surprise and said, "I don't understand one word you've said. I never gave you kings."

The entire group began to yell in confusion that the earth was full of kings, all of whom declared that they ruled with God's blessings.

"I don't know a thing about this!" God responded. "I created you all equal. I made you in my image. Good-bye!"

So ended the audience with God. But the deputies sat down in front of the gates of heaven and shed bitter tears. When God learned about this, he took pity on them and let them enter heaven again. Then he summoned an archangel and said, "Get the book in which I listed all of the plagues that were to fall upon human beings if they sinned, and check to see whether I wrote something about kings there."

The book was very thick, so the angel needed an entire day to complete his task. In the evening, when he was finished, he reported to the Lord that he had found nothing. So the deputies were led before God, who stated, "I don't know a thing about kings. Good-bye!"

The poor deputies became so desperate that God took pity on them once again. And again he summoned the angel and said to him, "Get the books in which I've recorded everything human beings must suffer for their foolish prayers so that they might learn that my teachings are wiser than theirs. Check to see whether I wrote anything about kings there."

And the angel did as he was commanded. However, since he had to read twelve thick books, it took him twelve days to finish the work. And he found nothing. So God granted the deputies an audience for the last time and said, "You'll have to return home without fulfilling your mission. There's nothing I can do for you. Kings are your own invention, and if you're sick and tired of them, then you must find your own way to get rid of them."

Edwin Hoernle

The Giant and His Suit of Armor

(1920)

nce upon a time there was a giant who had been captured by the hunchbacked dwarfs when he was very young. They made him their slave and forced him to plow the fields and weave clothes for them. He also had to grind wheat into flour for them, bake bread, slaughter animals, and cook. He chopped down trees in the woods and carried stones from the quarries to build their houses. From the earth he mined iron and gold. He watched over the ugly children of the dwarfs, carried them in his arms, washed their dirty diapers, and tolerated all of their moods. He was a hardworking, good-hearted giant.

Nevertheless, the hunchbacked masters forced him to wear heavy chains on his hands and feet. They beat him and pushed him around, cursed and mocked him to their heart's content. Whenever he prepared delicious meals with costly wine for their pleasure, they forced him to sit in a corner and chew on dry bread. The dwarfs wore clothes made of satin and silk, but the giant, who made their clothes, had to content himself with some dirty rags. While the dwarfs sat in comfortable rooms and slept in soft beds, which their large slave had built, the giant cowered in a miserable cave that was exposed to the scorching heat in summer and icy winds in winter. They were evil and hard masters, the hunchbacked dwarfs.

One time, in his youth, the giant had tried to break his chains. The dwarfs had beaten him nearly to pulp and had almost let him starve to death, and in response he rose and growled. He broke the chains, and the dwarfs fled in fear. But from the distance they shot arrows and threw spears at him. He lost so much blood that he fell unconscious to the ground. When he awoke, he was bound by more chains than ever before. Like a beaten dog, he crawled back into his cave.

In time the giant became older and thought more about his miserable situation. While he worked, he tried to figure out how everything had come to be the way it was. Of course, the dwarfs told him that this was the way things had always been and that they had never been different. But the giant was not satisfied with this answer.

Once, while he was working alone in the fields, a stranger passed by and told him that there were giants who lived on the other side of the mountain. They were twice as strong as he was, held their heads high, and enjoyed the fruits of their own work. The fact was that they were free and nobody's slaves. From that day on the giant's heart was filled with longing and resentment. Day and night he thought of ways to escape to the other side of the mountain.

The dwarfs were quick to notice that the giant had something up his sleeve. He often grumbled as he worked, talked to himself at length in the evening, and was particularly spiteful to one dwarf who had been bothering him. "We had better be on our guard," the dwarfs said, and they doubled the chains and posted more guards who were to keep an eye on the giant.

"How can I break through the ring of guards?" the giant asked himself. "I've got to make a suit of armor that will protect me against their arrows and spears." When night fell, he went into his cave and began to construct a suit of armor. The giant spent many evenings and nights bent over his work. Whenever it appeared that sleep might overcome him, he would pull himself together, slam his fist on the anvil, and cry, "I want to be free!" That was the way he encouraged himself and remained happy.

Once the dwarfs realized what he was doing, they entered his cave while he was asleep and destroyed the suit of armor. Afterward the giant was very depressed, but he did not lose hope. He concocted a new suit of armor, much stronger and harder than the old one, and the dwarfs were no longer able to damage it.

From then on the giant could only think and make plans about his suit of armor. He built a helmet and breastplate, protective slats for the back and shin guards, then a sharp sword. Sometimes an inner voice spoke to him: "Now's the time. Go to it! Break your chains! Put on your armor, take your sword, and rush through the ring of guards over the mountain!" But the giant was never sure that the time had come. There was always something to improve on the suit of armor. Or he thought the sword was too light or too heavy. Thus, the giant lost valuable time.

In the meantime the dwarfs were not idle. They built trenches around their entire country, created traps, and blocked passages with branches and hidden snares. They also poisoned their arrows so that just one hit would suffice to lame the giant. When they were finished, they began to sneer at the giant. They beat him and forced him to work harder than ever before. The giant bent his back, for he thought, "In case of an emergency I have my suit of armor." From then on he worked doubly hard on its completion.

Days, weeks, and years passed in this way. The more the dwarfs beat him, the more the giant thought, "Just wait!" And he threatened with his suit of armor. But he never put it on, though it had been finished for some time. However, now he felt that it was too precious to let it be shot at by the dwarfs. "I must preserve my suit of armor," the giant said, and he looked after it as though it were the apple of his eye.

Eventually, the giant forgot why he had actually created the suit of armor. He also forgot about the mountain and the country on the other side. He considered himself free because—well, he had the suit of armor. The clever dwarfs let him believe what he wanted to believe and laughed secretly whenever he threatened to do anything. They knew that the armor had become much too large and heavy for the giant to wear and carry over the mountain. Moreover, the sword had become blunt and jagged. "You're a very powerful giant," they said to their slave, and the giant never realized that they had gotten the better of him.

A rather foolish giant, don't you think?

Edwin Hoernle

The Little King and the Sun

(1920)

nce upon a time there was a little king who was annoyed that the sun rose over the mountains without much ado. So he commanded the sun to wait until he summoned it.

The sun paid no attention to him.

The little king became furious. He commanded his ministers to have chains and rope brought to him along with ten thousand soldiers. And the little king swore that he would tie the sun to the earth.

The sun climbed higher and higher.

The little king scrambled up the tower. He had a thousand cannons placed around the tower, and from its peak he cried out to the sun, "I'm greater than you!"

He took a lantern, lit it, and said, "And I shine as well."

But the sun climbed higher.

The woods below the king began to bustle.

The birds began to sing.

The animals appeared on the meadows sparkling in the morning dew and greeted the sun.

The little king trembled with fear and anger.

His subjects came out of their houses, gazed at the sun and at the little king high up on the tower. He fumed and yelled that he would kill anyone who dared to say that the sun was more powerful than he was.

The subjects were petrified.

But a little child began to laugh. A bunch of little children laughed. The entire troop of little children laughed. Then mothers also laughed; fathers, old people, girls, boys, and the oldest grandmothers laughed. Everyone laughed. The trees laughed, the animals laughed, the tiniest blades of grass laughed. The laughing of the people, animals, and grass mounted until it became like a violent, roaring storm.

And there were no longer any subjects!

The little king scampered down the stairs of his tower. And the king's henchmen hid quickly in their cellars. However, the people dragged them from their hiding places, bound them, and forced them to walk in the sun.

Thereafter, they all went about their daily work.

Except for the children, who ran into the meadows, danced, and sang.

And the sun smiled.

Berta Lask

The Boy Who Wanted to Fight with a Dragon

(1921)

 boy and a girl walked together on a country road. They were carrying books and pencils in their knapsacks and heading toward school. Along the way the boy said, "We have our history lesson today. That's neat! The teacher will tell us again how the Germans fought the French. I love to hear all about it. You know, when I grow up, I'll go to war and kill all the French."

The girl replied, "Please don't kill all of them. Perhaps there are some good people among them. Then you'll have killed the good with the bad."

But the boy answered, "What do you mean? There are no good ones. I'm going to kill them all."

They continued along their way for a while, and the young girl asked, "What sort of stories did your mother tell you? She knows so many."

The young boy said, "Yesterday she told me about Siegfried and how he killed a dragon. And the day before she told me about little Roland and how he killed a giant. You know, when I grow up, I'm going to kill a dragon and a giant or many dragons and giants. And there are evil knights who kidnap princesses and hold them prisoner. I'm going to kill all of the evil knights, too, and free all the princesses."

"That's terrific," the girl said. "And I'll help you."

The young boy laughed and said, "You want to help me? But you're just a girl. Girls can't kill dragons. Boys are the only ones who know how to do that."

Then the girl responded, "Well, you can at least show me the dragon after you've killed one. I want to see if it's a real one. Still, I'll do something that's just as good as killing dragons."

"What's that?" the boy asked.

"I don't know yet. I still have time."

Just at that moment they arrived in front of the school.

Several years later the young boy was grown up and no longer went to school. So he bought a gun and ammunition and marched along the country road—"left, right, left, right," snappy, like a soldier. He was now ready to fight against the French. But when he asked people where he could find the enemy forces of the French, they laughed at him and said, "The war with the French ended many years ago. There's nothing to fight against now."

When the young man heard this, he returned sadly to his home and placed the ammunition in a drawer and the gun in a closet. "I can't fight the French now," he thought, "but I can still kill a dragon and evil knights who kidnap princesses."

The following day the young man wandered along the country road again. He wore a fine suit made out of smooth blue cloth and a warm overcoat. Under the coat he carried a large sharp sword that he wanted to use to kill dragons and evil knights. After some time he arrived in a city. And as he went through the streets, he heard a soft clappety-clap. Hey, the young man thought, it clatters like iron armor. There must be a knight around here somewhere. And he listened carefully to the clattering noise that came out of a cellar. The young man crouched and looked through a window; he saw a young girl with a pale, sad face. Hey, the young man thought, she must be a princess. I'm going to go right down there and kill the iron knight and free the princess.

The young man went down some steps and entered a small, dark cellar. An old woman sat on a stool and peeled potatoes, and a sewing machine stood at the window. There sat the pale girl whom the young man had seen from outside. She was sewing as fast as she could and did not even look up at the young man as he entered. The young man was puzzled by this and said, "I thought you were a kidnapped princess because you looked so sad and pale, and I thought an evil knight was guarding you because I heard rattling like an iron armor."

You fool, the girl wanted to say, but then she stopped sewing for a moment and looked up at him. And when she noticed that his face was good and honest, the girl laughed a little and said, "My iron sewing machine is the evil knight that keeps me prisoner. I have to sew from early morning until late at night and can hardly leave the room. If it were a knight, it would fall asleep every now and then or die. But the sewing machine neither sleeps nor dies."

The young man then drew his sword from beneath his coat and said, "I'm going to chop the sewing machine into a thousand pieces so that it will no longer hold you prisoner."

But the girl became very annoyed and cried, "You foolish thing, if you destroy my sewing machine, my mother and I will starve."

"But what are you sewing?" the young man asked.

"I sew fine suits like the one you have on," the girl said.

"But why must you sit like a prisoner and work day and night in a small dark room?" the young man asked.

"I don't know why," the girl said. "I don't have time to trouble myself to find out why. But if you are a good, brave lad, then you could take the time and trouble to find out."

"Yes," the young man said. "I'll do it, and when I know how to help you, I'll return."

The young girl laughed again and then quickly continued to sew as the young man departed.

I'd rather fight against a knight than against a sewing machine, the young man thought, but now I don't know what I should do. And he continued on his way steeped in thought. After some time he left the city and came to a patch of woods. There, in the distance, he could see a large factory with two tall chimneys puffing thick, black smoke into the air. Suddenly women, girls, and little children emerged and headed toward the factory. The stragglers were running. Why are they running like that, the young man thought; perhaps there's a wild animal running after them, perhaps a dragon. And he called to the women, "Don't be afraid of the dragon. I'll handle him."

"What's that? What shouldn't we be afraid of?" the women asked.

"The dragon who's after you," the young man replied.

The women and girls laughed loudly. But one of the women went over to the young man. She led two children by the hand and told him, "There's no dragon after us. But there is a dragon in front of us, waiting for us. Do you see the flames coming out of his mouth?"

Through an open door of the factory the young man saw a gigantic furnace filled with glowing red coal. That was what the woman meant by flames coming out of the dragon's mouth.

"And do you see the black smoke he puffs out of his nose? That's the dragon. He drags me away from my children every day."

"Do you always have to go to the dragon?"

"Every day, from early morning until late at night."

"And what do you do there the entire day?"

"We make nice warm cloth like the cloth of your coat," the woman said.

"I don't want to wear a warm coat anymore if you have to leave your children alone because of it," the young man said. "I'm going to start a large fire and burn down the entire factory. Then the dragon won't be able to drag you away."

"No," the woman said, "that's the one thing you shouldn't do. Otherwise, my children and I shall starve. But if you're a smart, brave lad, think of a way you can help us."

Upon saying that, the woman went with the others into the factory. The children remained outside, and many cried because their mothers had gone away. Just then a young woman carrying a basket came out of the woods. It was the girl who had gone to school with the young man some years ago. Upon catching sight of the young woman, the children stopped crying and ran toward her. She began telling them beautiful stories, and she played with them. And when the children became hungry, she took some bread and milk from the basket so that they could eat and drink.

The young man was surprised and watched for some time. He no longer thought about the sword under his coat, and it slipped to the ground without his noticing it. But the young woman cried out to him, "You've lost your sword. Come over here, and bring it with you."

The young man turned around and said, "Let it lie there. I don't need it now."

The young woman laughed and asked him whether he had killed all of the dragons. "Why didn't you bring me one?"

"I haven't killed one single dragon yet," the young man said. "It's more difficult than I thought. The real dragon that causes evil keeps on hiding. But I'll find him one day, and then I'll fight it out with him."

Joachim Ringelnatz

Kuttel Daddeldu Tells His Children the Fairy Tale about Little Red Cap
(1923)

o kids, if you can keep your mouths shut for just five minutes, then I'll tell you the story about Little Red Cap if I can still make sense out of it. Old Captain Muckelmann told it to me long ago when I was still little and dumb like you are now. And Captain Muckelmann never lied.

So perk up your ears. There was once a little girl. She was dubbed Little Red Cap—that means, she was given the name because she wore a red cap on her head day and night. She was a beautiful girl, red as blood and white as snow, and black as ebony with large round eyes. From behind her legs were very thick and in front—well, to be brief, she was a hell of a beautiful, wonderful, fine lass.

And one day her mother sent her through the woods to grandmother who was, naturally, sick. And the mother gave Little Red Cap a basket with three bottles of Spanish wine and two bottles of Scotch and a bottle of Rostocker rye and a bottle of Swedish punch and a bottle of schnapps and some more bottles of beer and cake and all kinds of junk that was supposed to help the grandmother strengthen herself.

"Little Red Cap," the mother said extra. "Don't stray off the path, for there are wild wolves in the woods!" (The entire story must have taken place in Nikolayev or somewhere in Siberia.) Little Red Cap promised everything and took off. And the wolf met her in the woods.

Joachim Ringelnatz, "Kuttel Daddeldu Tells His Children the Fairy Tale about Little Red Riding Cap" (private manuscript, 1923). Illustrator: Joachim Ringelnatz.

"Little Red Cap," he asked, "where are you going?" And she told him everything you already know. And he asked, "Where does your grandmother live?"

And she told him the exact address, "Schwieger Strasse thirteen, ground floor."

And then the wolf showed the child where there were juicy raspberries and strawberries and enticed her from the path deep into the woods.

And while she busily picked berries, the wolf ran full-sail ahead to Schwieger Strasse, number thirteen, and knocked on the door of the ground floor at Grandmother's place.

The grandmother was a suspicious old woman with many holes in her teeth. That's why she asked rudely, "Who's knocking there at my door?"

And outside, the wolf answered in a disguised voice, "It's me, Sleeping Beauty."

And then the old woman called out, "Come in!" And the wolf swept into the room. And then the old woman put on her nightgown and bonnet and ate the wolf all up.

In the meantime Little Red Cap had lost her way in the woods. And she was just like most dim-witted girls; she began to bawl. And the hunter heard her deep in the woods and rushed to her side. Well—and what does it matter to us what the two of them wanted to do there deep in the woods since it had become very dark in the meantime. At any rate he did bring her to the right path.

So she ran to Schwieger Strasse. And there she saw that her grandmother had become fat and bloated.

And Little Red Cap asked, "Grandmother, why do you have such big eyes?" And the grandmother answered, "That's so I can see you better!"

And Little Red Cap asked again, "Grandmother, why do you have such big ears?"

And the grandmother answered, "That's so I can hear you better!"

And then Little Red Cap asked again, "Grandmother, why do you have such a big mouth?"

Joachim Ringelnatz, "Kuttel Daddeldu Tells His Children the Fairy Tale about Little Red Riding Cap" (private manuscript, 1923). Illustrator: Joachim Ringelnatz.

Joachim Ringelnatz, "Kuttel Daddeldu Tells His Children the Fairy Tale about Little Red Riding Cap" (private manuscript, 1923). Illustrator: Joachim Ringelnatz.

Now is that the right thing for children to say to a grown-up grandmother?

So the old woman became so stark raving mad that she couldn't utter one more word. Instead she ate Little Red Cap all up, and then she moved like a whale.

Just then the hunter passed by outside, and he wondered how a whale could have landed in Schwieger Strasse. So he loaded his rifle and drew his long knife out of its sheath and entered the room without knocking. And there to his horror he saw the bloated grandmother in bed instead of the whale.

And—diavolo caracho! You'll be wiped off your feet! It's hard to believe—but the gluttonous old woman ate up the hunter too.

Yeah, you brats are gaping with wide-open mouths, waiting for something more to come. But clear out of here now quick as the wind; otherwise I'll tan your hides.

My throat's become completely dry from these dumb, stinking stories, which are only all lies anyway.

March yourselves out of here! Let your father pour one down the hatch now, you leftover small fry!

Hermynia Zur Mühlen

The Fence

(1924)

nce upon a time there was a large island in the middle of a mighty, turbulent blue sea. The soil of this island was extremely fertile, so everything grew as if by itself. The people had no worries, nor did they suffer. They lived from the fruits of the earth that seemed to fall into their laps. They owned all sorts of domestic animals: cows, which gave them milk; sheep, which gave them wool; and chickens, which gave them eggs. Everything was the common property of everyone else, so nobody suffered from need or neglect.

Each inhabitant of the island owned a small cottage. Whenever food or clothing was needed, one went to the animal stalls or to the large hall on the seashore where the women spun, wove, and worked. Each person had only to go there, show some worn or torn clothing, and say, "I need some new clothes," and they were delivered on the spot. If a person had helped tend the animals, fed them, and cut their wool, he or she had a right to their wool.

The people lived very happily on their splendid island, and life was a daily festival, especially for the children. However, among the inhabitants of the island there were good and evil people, generous and greedy people, like everywhere. Among the greedy people there was a small hunchbacked man by the name of Grabit. He was particularly annoyed because all of the other people were just as rich as he was and because he had to help till the common fields and tend the animals just like everyone else. For a long time he thought of a way in which he could begin to change this situation, and finally it seemed as though he had worked out a plan because he became happy and cheerful, and his face, which had always been sullen, took on a bright expression.

All of the people had small gardens around their cottages. Depending on their taste, they planted vegetables or flowers, and anyone who planted vegetables was allowed to take flowers from the neighbor's garden to decorate his cottage. In return the other person fetched vegetables from his neighbor's garden.

One day Grabit went into the forest and chopped some wood, which he dragged home. He worked during moonlight, and in the morning there was a high fence around his garden with a small door that could be locked from the inside. When the islanders caught sight of the fence, they were astonished and stopped in their tracks. They had never seen such a thing before, and they did not understand its purpose.

"A strange decoration," one man stated. "I think it looks real ugly."

"No," a woman declared. "I like it. It's so orderly."

Some laughed while others stood and admired the artful door. However, nobody had an inkling about what the whole thing meant.

Grabit had a friend, the strongest, biggest, and also the dumbest man on the island, a stocky fellow who could not think for himself and who believed everything he was told. One day Grabit summoned this man to him and asked, "Do you want to become richer and happier than anyone else?"

The blockhead nodded. "Why not, if it won't exhaust me." Not only was he dumb, but he was also very lazy.

"It won't be especially troublesome for you," the sly Grabit said. "You only have to say that I'm right, no matter what I do, and if anyone attacks me, you must protect me."

"I'll gladly do that." The blockhead laughed, for he thought to himself, Nobody on our island attacks anyone else. I won't have to exhaust myself with much protection.

Grabit took a large, sharp knife from a hiding place and gave it to the blockhead. "I want you to carry this with you constantly, and if I call you, I want you to come and protect me with this weapon."

The following night Grabit went to the animal stalls and henyards of the community. He took two cows and twelve hens and drove them into his garden behind the fence. When the islanders passed by Grabit's garden the next morning and saw the animals behind the fence, they laughed because they believed it was all a joke. But when the time came for the women to fetch milk for their children, they did not have enough because the milk of the two cows that Grabit had driven into his garden was missing. So the women went to the fence and cried out, "Grabit, let us in. We want to milk the cows."

However, Grabit stood behind the closed door and yelled to the women, "What's the idea? Don't you see that the cows are in my garden? Whatever is in my garden behind the fence belongs to me, and you're not allowed to touch it."

The women thought that Grabit had lost his mind, and they called their men to help them. But Grabit said the same thing to them, and he added, "Two nights ago an angel descended from heaven and said to me, 'Grabit, whatever lies behind your fence is your property, and property is holy. Whoever dares to touch your property must die.' Therefore, take care and keep away from my cows and chickens, otherwise heaven will punish you. And there's more I want to show you!" With these words he shoved Blockhead into the open. "This man is carrying a sharp knife, and he will kill anyone who touches my property."

Since the islanders really believed that an angel had descended from heaven, they became sad, and they also feared the sharp knife and powerful fists of the blockhead. So they lowered their heads and trudged despondently toward their homes. Only a few women, whose children had not received milk, remained and complained loudly in front of the fence, "Grabit, our children are crying for milk. What should we do?"

"I'm a good man," Grabit answered, "and I'm concerned about your innocent children. Still, property is holy, and, if I were to give you the milk from my cows for nothing, that would ruin their holiness. Work a few hours longer each day and bring me some beautiful clothes; then I'll give you milk in exchange."

Since the women had no other way to obtain the milk, they obeyed. From then on there was more than one occasion when the islanders awoke and saw another new fence around another garden, and behind the fence there would be cows, chickens, and sheep. And each time the man who built the fence explained that an angel had also come to him and had spoken the same words he had spoken to Grabit. And each time one of the men hired one of the eleven brothers of Blockhead, gave him a large sharp knife, and ordered him to protect his property.

Ultimately, everything on the island belonged to just twelve men, who lived in great harmony with one another and enjoyed comfortable lives. The rest of the islanders had to work for them and received only half of what they used to earn. The twelve men commanded the twelve blockheads to build a stone house with iron bars, and all of those who tried to take something from the property of the twelve men were imprisoned there.

Now there was misery and sadness on the island, and when the people passed Grabit's fence, they clenched their fists and muttered, "Cursed fence, everything has turned against us since you came. If we had only torn you down the first day we saw you!" But they only said this softly, for the blockheads stood on watch, and each word said against Grabit and his friends was punished severely.

The blockheads received all they wanted to eat and wore green clothes, which were more beautiful than those worn by the other islanders. Soon many men who could no longer bear looking at their starving children sold themselves to the twelve rich men, joined the ranks of the blockheads, and fought against their brothers.

Actually, the islanders would not have tolerated the rule of the twelve men if they had not really believed that an angel had come from heaven and declared that property was holy. The twelve men also wrote a thick book of commandments that dealt largely with the holiness of property. Whoever did not follow the commandments was to be severely punished.

That was the way things were, and they became worse and worse. Then one day a ship arrived from another island, where fences, holy property, and blockheads with sharp knives did not exist. The strangers came on land, and since they were friendly people, the islanders told them about their misery.

"Why don't you defend yourselves?" the strangers asked.

"An angel brought the holy law," the islanders explained and looked shyly to see if the strangers understood their problem. However, the strangers laughed so loud that their laughter sounded like thunder, and all of the fences on the island began to tremble. Then they declared, "You fools, don't you realize that Grabit and his eleven friends are thieves. They've stolen what belonged to all of you, and they've protected their stolen goods with fences. Their holy laws are the laws of crooks, and the blockheads who protect the stolen goods are also plain crooks. Come with us. We'll help you recover what they've stolen from you."

Now it dawned on the islanders how blind they had been. The men ran to fetch their hoes and axes. The strangers took out their knives. Soon the fences were smashed and torn to the ground on the entire island. Eleven of the rich men became so horrified that they returned the stolen goods and promised to work again and to stop stealing. Grabit, however, defended himself and was killed by the strangers. The blockheads ran away and hid in the forest.

When the strangers sailed homeward on their ships, they left behind them a happy and cheerful island where hunger and misery no longer existed and where it became impossible for a thief to use sly lies to make himself into a ruler over others.

Hermynia Zur Mühlen

The Servant
(1923)

nce upon a time there was a small village at the foot of a huge mountain deep in the wilderness, somewhat isolated from the rest of the world. The tiny village was poor. Icy winds roared down from the mountain and killed everything that was planted in the region. Moreover, the fields of the villagers were sandy and unfertile, so living conditions were dreadful. Only one thing was plentiful—wood. There was more than enough wood. Gigantic trees grew on the side of the mountain, and on the other side of the village there was an endless forest. The villagers chopped down the trees, sold the beautiful thick logs to the world outside, and obtained just what they needed to exist.

However, this work was hard. When the men cut the trees in the boiling summer, the heat practically killed them. When they dragged the logs on their sleds in the chilly winter, their hands and feet froze. All this terribly hard work made them sullen and bad-tempered, and one rarely heard a happy laugh or cheerful word in the little village.

In the middle of the forest there was a cabin, the home of an old man and his son. The villagers were frightened of the man. They thought he was a magician because the cabin was filled with strange instruments, and the man worked day and night on a tremendously large thing that seemed to move by itself. It puffed out steam and rumbled loudly. The children were scared of the cabin, and even the grown-ups avoided the magician, for they were afraid that he could do them some harm. But they were unfair to the magician, for he was actually a good and clever man who was touched deeply by the misery of his fellow creatures. He wanted to help them so that they would not have to work so terribly hard. He saw how much trouble it was to cut the thick logs with a paltry tiny saw. He saw how the men had to drudge, how laborious the work was, and he made up his mind to invent a machine that would be so easy to handle that even a small child could work it.

The magician toiled many, many years in his cabin. By the time his work was finally finished, he had become gray and old. He looked at the machine with great joy, folded his trembling hands in his lap, and told his son to call the men of the village to their cabin. Since their curiosity was greater than their fear, the men came. When they were all gathered together, the son of the magician carried an enormous oak stump into the room and placed it under the large machine. The magician touched a switch, and the machine began to hum loudly and puff little white clouds. A gigantic saw fell on the clump of oak wood, moved back and forth a few times—whrrrr, whrrrr, whrrrr, whrrrr—and the clump of oak wood split apart as though it were but a thin little branch. The men were astonished, and at first they stood there speechless, but after a while they began to overwhelm the old magician with questions.

"I've created a servant for you," the old man explained, "and this servant will help you with your work. It's not right when people must work so hard they have no time to be cheerful. Since the servant can accomplish in a few hours what it takes you entire days to do, you'll have time to play with your children and speak with your wives. You'll no longer have to work as hard as beasts."

And then he showed the men how to use the large saw, and it was so simple that a ten-year-old boy could understand everything. The men shouted with joy and could scarcely find words enough to thank the magician. However, he raised his hand in warning and spoke some serious words to them.

"I'm giving you this servant as a present, but make sure that the servant does not become your master, for he would be a cruel master and would swallow the lives of your kin and kindred."

The men laughed and cried out, "You want to make fools out of us! How could a lifeless thing made out of iron and leather become the master of living human beings?"

The old magician looked at them with concern and then spoke, "As long as this servant belongs to *all of you,* he will be a good servant and will help you. However, if one day he should belong to one person alone, he will become a wicked master. Thus, I want you to promise me that the servant will always belong to the entire village." He turned to his son. "You shall be the guardian of the servant. You shall allow anyone in the village to use it whenever it is needed. As long as you do this faithfully, my blessings as your father shall be with you. If the servant should fall into the hands of a single person through your fault, you and your children and your grandchildren shall be cursed!"

The men promised the old magician that the servant would always remain the property of the entire community and that no one person would dare to keep it for himself alone. However, secretly they laughed at the old man and his warning. "He's already become senile," the eldest of the villagers remarked to the others. "You would think that there's some magic power in the saw that could make it into our master. The old fool!" Even the magician's son did not fully grasp his father's words, and he scoffed at the old man along with the others. Still, they took good care to conceal their thoughts from the magician, for they were afraid that he might take back his present.

It seemed that the good old magician had lived only to complete his work. Just a few days after he had given the servant as a gift to the men of the village, he lay down and died. But before he closed his eyes for good, he repeated his warning; his last word were "Beware that the servant does not become your master!"

Soon happy times arrived for the village. The work that had taken the men many days to complete was done by the servant in a few hours. Since the villagers did not have to work themselves to death to earn a living and could now enjoy some hours of rest, they became cheerful and were in good spirits. Laughter and joking could be heard throughout the village. The people were no longer so tired, and they no longer felt pains in their arms and legs. Consequently, they became kinder and tenderer toward one another, and their town became known to everyone in the region as the "happy village." Many people came from distant lands to settle there because it was more beautiful than anywhere else in the world.

The magician's son was a good, simple fellow. He looked after his father's present faithfully and was content because he saw how the village had become happy and prosperous, and he even laughed at times when he thought about his father's warning. The servant worked industriously, huffing and puffing, obeying each and every touch of the hand. How could the old magician have ever believed that this mass of matter could become a master?

Many years passed in happiness. Then one day a stranger appeared in the village. He was dressed in beautiful and elegant clothes, wore a golden chain over his fat stomach, jingled gold coins in his pockets, and told stories about splendid things he had seen in the great wide world. His arrogance irritated the villagers, and they wanted to prove to him that they were not poor wretches and that they possessed something that nobody else in the world possessed. So they took him to the huge shed they had built for the servant, and they showed him how beautifully and quickly the machine worked. The stranger's eyes and mouth opened wider and wider the longer he looked at the servant. However, he did not say a word but sat down silently in a corner, sunk deep in thought.

That evening he knocked on the door of the cabin where the magician's son lived, and when he was let in, he explained that he wanted to buy the servant.

"That's impossible," the young man replied. "We had to promise my father never to allow the servant to fall into the hands of a single person."

The stranger drew a handful of gold from his pocket. "Look here. With this you can travel all over the world. You can become a great man and wear beautiful clothes with a golden chain."

The young man looked sadly at the gold. He would have liked to become a rich, stately man; however, he did not dare break his promise. The stranger spent a long time trying to talk him into it, but the young man remained firm and kept giving the stranger the same answer: "I can't." But secretly he cursed the folly of his father who had robbed him of this chance to make a great fortune.

On the following day the stranger called all the men of the village together in the large shed, and he threw two large handfuls of gold on the ground and said, "Sell me the servant!"

"We can't!" they cried out unanimously, but some of the men looked greedily at the gold and thought, The old magician is dead, and it's impossible for him to know everything we're doing now—why shouldn't we sell the servant?

"Listen to me," the stranger said, "The servant will remain in your village and continue to work here. Everything will be much better for you than ever before because I'll give you work, and each week you'll receive a salary. You won't have to wait until the wood is transported. I'll take over all your problems, all your burdens, because I care for you. And every week you'll receive your money. Don't be fools. You see that I'm a good man and only want the best for you."

The village eldest scratched his ear and looked at the others. Then he walked up to the stranger, looked straight into his eyes, and said, "I see that you're a man to be trusted, a man concerned about the welfare of our village. Allow me to shake your hand."

And he shook the stranger's hand tightly. When he withdrew his hand from the stranger's, the village eldest clenched his fist, for he could already feel the beautiful, hard gold coins in his hand.

Once again the stranger raised his voice. "Look, men, you are simple inexperienced people. You've always sold the wood for the same price. Yet because of my brains, I understand how to force people to pay much more for the wood than they do now, double, perhaps even triple."

"But," the magician's son exclaimed with concern, "If you just give us the same salary all the time, what benefit do we have when you get more money for the wood?"

The stranger shook his head sadly and responded, "Oh, my poor friends, how dumb you are! The time will come when nobody will want to buy wood anymore. Then I'll stand there with huge amounts of wood and my pockets empty. In spite of this, you'll continue to take your salaries home each week."

He rubbed the tears from his eyes with a silk handkerchief, and his voice trembled with emotion. "Perhaps I shall become a poor man, but I love people so much, and especially you all, that it doesn't matter to me. I see how much trouble you have in transporting the wood, and I want to relieve you of this burden. It pains my heart when I think that your earnings are so unsteady. I'd have to give you a steady salary; otherwise my heart would break." And the noble stranger began to shed bitter tears.

Now the village eldest stepped forward and spoke to the men. He declared that the stranger was right and that they were fools if they didn't sell him the servant. This man knew how to persuade the people, and after a short time they all exclaimed, "Let's sell the servant!"

Only the magician's son remained sadly in a corner. His good, simple mind did not know what it was that troubled him, but he was shaking from a terrible fear, and he shouted, "You can't sell the servant. I won't allow it!" And he leaped forward and tried to grab the stranger's throat.

But the stranger managed to yell, "You see now who your enemy is! I'm offering you a beautiful secure life, and he wants to prevent you from having this! Seize him!"

The men surrounded the young man and held him tightly.

"As long as this wicked man lives here," the stranger continued, "there will be no peace in this village. Send him away, and if he should dare to return, beat him to death!"

The men dragged the magician's son to the outskirts of the village and then drove him with sticks into the forest. The young man cried and screamed wildly, "The servant will become your master! The servant will become your master!"

Soon after the stranger had acquired the servant, he became a totally different person. No longer did he speak kind words. Instead, he ordered the men about, yelled at them, and never let them have their say. The work was now divided. Some of the men toiled in the large shed, some hauled the logs to the shed, and some had to carry the wood from the village. And this went on from dusk to dawn. If someone became tired or sick and informed the stranger that he couldn't work that day, the stranger would bellow, "Good, then you won't receive your salary." And the sick man would groan and drag himself to work.

At first, despite everything, the men were happy and in good spirits because they received a steady salary

Hermynia Zur Mühlen, *Ali, der Teppichweber* (Berlin: Malik, 1923). Illustrator: John Heartfeld. Tale: "The Servant."

each week. But soon they realized that this salary was not enough to live on. The stranger had a mansion built for himself in the village, and many people from the city came and settled in the region. When the mansion was finished, one of the workers approached the stranger and said, "You're a rich man. You must certainly have sold the wood for triple the price. Otherwise you wouldn't have been able to have this castle built for yourself. Yet our salaries have remained the same, and I think that you should now give us triple our salary."

The stranger became furious. He called his twelve armed guards, whom he had brought with him from the city, and he had the worker hung from a tree. The others who saw this became very frightened and no longer dared to say a word, for they had no weapons.

The stranger had a larger whistle installed in the great steel room where the servant now stood. When this whistle piped shrilly each morning, the men had to rush to work or they would not receive their salaries. One morning when one of the men was still asleep, the whistle shrieked, and his small son shook him until he woke. Then the boy said anxiously, "Hurry, hurry, father. The master is calling!" The father looked at the small boy in dismay, for he recalled the words of the old magician. That evening he told his comrades about the incident, and the men sighed and had to admit that the servant had truly become their master, and they were his slaves.

The happy village had become a sad one again. Nobody had time to be nice to anyone else. Nobody laughed anymore. Everyone was sullen and tired. The stranger had a tremendous building constructed next to the steel shed. Here matches were made out of wood, and even small children were obliged to work. The women had long since begun working because the families could not live from the meager wages of the men alone.

One day many men arrived in the village from distant places, and the stranger gave them lodging in two large houses that had been empty for some time. The villagers were astonished and asked why these men had come—they did not look for work and appeared to be waiting for something to happen. This question was soon answered. The stranger called the workers to him, made a sad face, and said, "I have suffered great losses, and because of my concern for your welfare, I've become a poor man. Wood now costs just half of what it used to cost. So I can only give you half your salary from now on."

The workers were horrified and looked at each other. They could hardly live on their salaries as it was, and now they were to receive just half their pay. One worker, a young man, stepped forward and yelled so loud that he became red with rage: "We won't work for half our salary!"

The stranger grinned and sneered. "What do you want to do then? Do you want to cut the logs with your miserable little saws? Before you've cut up one tree, the servant will have cut ten or more. You can't compete against the servant—and the machine is in my hands!"

Still, the workers were aroused by their furious anger, and they yelled wildly and in confusion: "We won't work! We won't work!"

The stranger's lips formed an evil smile, and he laughed. "Good, I don't need you. The men who recently came to the village will work instead. There's no longer any place for you now!"

The workers rushed forward and wanted to kill the stranger. But he blew a shrill little whistle, and suddenly there were many heavily armed men in the room. They surrounded the workers and tied them up. Then the stranger shouted in a mighty voice to the armed men: "Drive these troublemakers out of the village and guard the borders. Whoever comes near the borders is to be shot on sight!"

And so that is the way things happened. The men were driven into the woods with their wives and children just as they had once driven away the magician's son. As darkness descended, they sank exhaustedly to the moist ground, and the women sobbed and cried the entire night. "The servant has become our master! The servant has become our master!"

The next morning they wandered sadly and moved deeper into the forest. Tired and hungry, they dragged themselves the whole day long. Toward evening they reached a small cabin, and when they knocked on the door, the magician's son opened it and let them in. He welcomed them with tenderness, gave them beets and bread to eat, and took care of the crying children. The parents related what had happened and complained about their suffering.

"Now everything is lost," an old man moaned. "The servant has become our master, and we and our children and our grandchildren shall be his slaves forever."

"If only your father had never given us this unholy present!" another man cried. "We are much worse off now than ever before."

However, the magician's son became very serious and said, "Do not slander my father. Whatever he did, he did out of love for you, and his gift was good and useful as long as it belonged to everyone. Only when it fell into the hands of a single person did it become a curse. However, you should not lose heart even now. Think about the times when the servant helped us all. Weren't they happy and wonderful times?"

"Yes, yes!" they all exclaimed and sighed deeply as they thought about the time when their village had been called the "happy village."

"Why did you allow a single person to take over the servant?" a twelve-year-old boy cried. "We children would have believed the words of the magician, and we wouldn't have done that."

The old people became ashamed and silent, but the face of the magician's son glowed and beamed brightly all of a sudden. With a cheerful voice he declared, "During the past years I read a good deal in my father's magic books, and I constantly came across a saying that I had difficulty understanding until now. The saying goes like this:

"Whatever old people throw away, the young will pick up and keep.

"Whatever the old people do wrong, the young will do right.

"The master of the old people will become the servant of the young."

For a moment there was silence in the small cabin. Then all of the children rejoiced and shouted with their fresh young voices, "We'll make up for everything you've done wrong! Your master will become our servant!"

And the tall serious pine trees rustled softly and whispered, "That's the way, that's the way!"

Béla Balázs

The Victor

(1922)

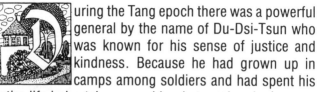uring the Tang epoch there was a powerful general by the name of Du-Dsi-Tsun who was known for his sense of justice and kindness. Because he had grown up in camps among soldiers and had spent his entire life in brutal wars and hard struggles, he became stronger than any other man, but he had a great yearning for a woman's warm love and tender care. One day he heard that the king of the Land of Four Rivers wanted to marry off his daughters and had called all of the distinguished warriors to his court. The king announced that they were to fight with one another, and he would give the three princesses as wives to the three victors. Du-Dsi-Tsun decided to leave his camp immediately and take part in the tournament, for the princesses were reputed to be unusually beautiful. And in addition to their beauty, they were known for being tender and kind. Therefore, Du-Dsi-Tsun got on his horse and rode to the castle of the king.

When Du-Dsi-Tsun arrived, the tournament had already ended. The three princesses were just being fetched from the ladies' chamber where they had been awaiting the outcome behind silk curtains so as not to hear the wild noise of the battle. They were about to offer their hands to the three victors as Du-Dsi-Tsun came riding through the gate.

"Wait for me," he called, still in his saddle. "I'm General Du-Dsi-Tsun, and I also want to fight for the king's daughters. I grew up among soldiers in the field. My entire life has been spent in brutal battles and hard struggles. My heart has great yearning for a woman's warm love and tender care."

When the king heard this, he allowed the tournament to begin again. This time the three princesses did not return to the ladies' chamber but sat down under the pillars of jade and watched. They appeared so delicate and beautiful between the slim pillars that the general thought they were like love songs that sleep between the strings of a harp.

"Which one do you want to fight for?" asked the king.

"For the eldest," replied Du-Dsi-Tsun, for he noticed that she was looking at him with ardent love in her eyes.

The battle began, and Du-Dsi-Tsun cut off the arm of his opponent at their first clash. When this warrior fell to the ground and rolled over moaning and crying in the dust, Du-Dsi-Tsun approached the eldest princess to take her hand. But the princess had stood up and looked at the defeated warrior with tears and pity in her eyes.

"You are to become my wife," the general said to her. "I saw the glow of love in your eyes."

But the princess lifted her tearful face, and her eyes had lost their glow and had become dim. "Du-Dsi-Tsun," she said, "you are victorious and strong. You don't need warm and loving care. But this poor man, who has become a helpless cripple because of me, what will happen to him if he doesn't have a woman to look after him?"

Du-Dsi-Tsun understood the justice of these words and turned to the king. "I want to fight for the second princess," he said.

At the first clash he cut off the right foot of his opponent and approached the second princess to receive his reward. But she cried aloud out of pity and ran to the wounded man.

"Du-Dsi-Tsun," she sobbed, "you're victorious and strong. But this unfortunate man has lost his foot. What will happen to him if he doesn't have a woman to take care of him?"

Du-Dsi-Tsun understood the justice of these words.

He bit his lips and cried, "I want to fight for the third princess."

Now the general's passion flared up so powerfully in his heart that he cut off his opponent's head from the rest of his body at the first clash. Then he approached the third princess, who stood pale as death between the slim pillars of jade. She was silent and lowered her eyes, which were covered by long lashes.

"You are to be my wife," the general announced. "I won."

After a long silence the young princess replied, "You are victorious and strong, Du-Dsi-Tsun. But the soul of this murdered man cannot wrap itself in widow's weeds as in heavy, dark velvet, and now it floats around in the nocturnal winds like a torn feather."

Then she concealed her face and went away. General Du-Dsi-Tsun got on his horse and rode off into the distance. When he reached the edge of the wilderness, he dismounted and chased his horse away. Then he went alone into wilderness, where he wandered about and moaned loudly. After cursing his strength, he hung himself on the first tree he saw.

The Patched Pants

(1928)

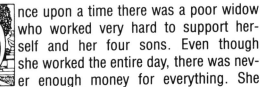nce upon a time there was a poor widow who worked very hard to support herself and her four sons. Even though she worked the entire day, there was never enough money for everything. She worked as a maid, and she also washed the dirty clothes of other people. Nevertheless, poverty was often an unwelcome guest in her small flat. There's a saying that hunger makes for the best kind of cook. Yet when there is hardly a thing in the home and four hungry mouths to feed, one can gladly do without such a cook. If a child cries, "Mother, I'm hungry," it's often like sweet music to a mother's ears, but only when the cupboard is full, when bread and potatoes are aplenty. However, if the last bread crumb has been eaten and there's no money to buy more bread, the child's hungry cry is enough to break the mother's heart.

Still, she tried to smile. "Soon, children, soon." Yes, that was often the way things were in the widow's home. Whenever it was at all possible, she made sacrifices so that her boys would have something to eat. But that's not all. The boys had to be clothed, and that caused certain problems. The oldest son had the best of the bargain. The youngest, who was six, had the worst, for he had to wear whatever was left over. So anything that wasn't torn into a thousand shreds made its way from Henry down to Johnny and Walter and finally to Frankie, whose suit often appeared to be made out of tiny patches. And his last pair of pants was truly a sort of miraculous patchwork.

Those rips and holes caused by Henry, Johnny, and

Walter were repaired, but Frankie added his own, for a fence is a fence and doesn't ask if the pants are strong and durable. And a young boy doesn't pay attention when he romps around and jumps all over the place. "Oh no, the pants!" Frankie's mother could only sigh when the pants came home with new rips and holes in them.

"Oh God, oh God, there's hardly a place for a new patch, and the stuff is already quite worn out!"

You can see that the pants were a sad lot. And Frankie had to suffer a great deal because some stupid children made fun of him and his pants. Sometimes he wished that he had been a girl to see whether his mother could have made a skirt out of the leftover pants. But he only thought about this and would have never said it to his mother.

The boys spent most of their free time on the streets. Every now and then they found ways to earn a little money by moving pushcarts or similar things. Once, when they were running around near a marketplace, they passed a junk store. An old man with a long white beard stood in front of the store. On his right shoulder sat a green parrot, and on the left, a multicolored parrot. The green one screeched:

Come right in,
fat and thin,
come right in!

And the multicolored parrot exclaimed:

Sell your junk!
Buy our junk!
Come right in,
and bargain,
bargain!

Just as little Frankie and his brothers rushed past the store, the two birds began to squeal and jump up and down excitedly on the old man's shoulders. "Come right in, come right in!" The screeching scared the children, and they ran faster. But the old man raced after them; with the parrots flying around his head as he ran. The boys were now more frightened and tried to run even faster. However, the junk dealer came closer and closer. Where could they find a hiding place? Suddenly, they spied an open door in an old abandoned house. The children scampered through the door with the junk dealer on their heels and the parrots crying:

Stay,
Oh, stay!
Just one word.
Don't run away.
Stay.
Don't run away!

The parrots sounded so sad that the boys calmed down. There were tears in the old man's eyes. "Children, children," he called to his parrots, "which one is it?"

The two parrots began to exclaim, "Frankie, Frankie!"

"Come with me," he said to the boys, "and I'll give you whatever you want."

The boys didn't know whether they should laugh or cry out for help. Finally, they summoned up the courage to go with the man. The two parrots flew ahead. The old man walked behind them, and the boys marched in the middle until they reached the store. The old man took his place in front of the door, and the two parrots screeched again. The green one cried,

Come right in,
fat and thin,
Come right in!

And the multicolored parrot added:

Sell your junk!
Buy our junk!
Come right in,

and bargain,
bargain!

The old man waved his hand, and the boys entered the store somewhat hesitantly. The air was stuffy and musty. There were old clothes, porcelain figures, bed frames, rusted pistols, pictures, watches, chains, glass pearls. A mess of junk, all mixed up, even shoes that had been totally worn out. Suddenly all of these things began to babble in confusion. There were so many sad stories to hear. Much trouble, much misery. And yet much love, yes, much love. The pair of shoes that had been completely worn out had experienced many different things. Up the stairs, down the stairs, early in the morning. Getting children ready for school and delivering papers, then cleaning the houses of other people. Once when it snowed outside, the shoes became soaking wet, and the poor old woman caught a cold and died. Since every little thing had to be sold to pay for the funeral, the old shoes went too.

That was only one of the stories. The bed frame told how it had been exchanged for a small coffin. The dancing porcelain figures that appeared so graceful with their uplifted skirts had seen better days. The silver watch had been exchanged for bread because a jobless father did not have enough money to feed his children. And he had been very proud of the watch when he received it as a present in his youth. He must have taken it out of his pocket over a thousand times and had been happy as a king to tell someone the correct time. And the golden chain in the junk store blinked sadly. It was difficult to see that it had been spotted by blood. Someone had been murdered because of this golden ornament. But my tale would be endless if I were to tell you all of the stories behind all of the things in the junk store.

The old man approached the boys and said, "They're all sad stories." The parrots flapped their wings. "And my story is also very sad. Once I was rich, but I never

Bruno Schönlank, *Der Kraftbonbon und andere Großstadtmärchen* (Berlin: Büchergilde Gutenberg, 1928).
Illustrator unknown. Tale: "The Patched Pants."

thought about anyone else's problems. I hired poor people to work for me, and I barely gave them enough so that they could eat. Oh yes, the people called me rich, but now I know just how poor I really was. Once a frail woman came to me and asked me for money because her children were starving.

"'I'll give you this old painting for the money,' she said.

"'Leave me alone,' I said, for I had very little time and was about to go to a dance. Then my two daughters cried out.

"'Come, father, come. We'll be late for the ball. Tell the old woman to go away.'

"'Sir,' the old woman said. 'Listen. It's for my children's sake. It's for my children!'

"'Don't bother me with your junk!' I shouted and shoved the woman aside. Then she touched my shoulders with her bony hands and looked at me with her large, hard eyes.

"'Well, then learn what junk really is!'

"And I felt myself becoming old, and my daughters were changed into parrots.

"So now I've been buying and selling junk for years. I feel that I'm getting older and older, and there's still no salvation."

And he began to weep so much that his tears fell onto the dusty floor.

"Who knows how long I must keep this up? But I must keep buying and selling until I find the most precious thing in the world. I've learned that the most precious thing is not jewelry or gold. No, it's invisible. The old and miserable things are often more precious than all of the splendors of the world. There's so much love and care, so much suffering and grief tied up with the old things."

The parrots flapped their wings again and called out, "Come, Frankie, give us your pants as a gift."

And Frankie looked at the patched pants, and suddenly the pants began to speak: "Think of how much love has been sewn into me. The gray patch there came from Henry. Do you remember how he slipped and tore a large hole in me? Your mother didn't scold him. She merely sighed, and then late in the evening she sewed the gray patch on me with her weary hands. Yes, you boys ripped many things, but fortunately you've stayed healthy and happy."

Then the patches and stitches began to speak. Stitch, stitch, stitch, stitch on summer evenings. Stitch, stitch, stitch, stitch on cold winter nights. Brrr, brrr, how cold, and yet the mother's hardworking hands toiled for the boys in the evenings, even when they were tired and worn out.

All of the satin and silk, all of the splendors of the earth are not enough to match this. The parrots landed on Frankie's shoulders and begged sadly: "Give us your pants as a gift!"

Frankie had now become fond of his pants, but when he looked at the parrots, he became so sorry for them that he said, "All right, they're yours."

And as he began to take off his pants, he heard wonderful and enchanting music. All of a sudden, two large, beautiful girls appeared and tenderly embraced him and his brothers. And the old man became a strong and healthy man again.

"Come, my boys," he said. "Let's go to your flat."

And the boys raced home followed by the man and his daughters, and when their mother returned that evening, she was astonished by what she saw. However, the man said, "We want to live with you and work together. That way we can make things easier for each other. I and my daughters have learned a great deal, so we can help chase away the problems in your home."

The people in the entire building gathered together in the courtyard, and there was a huge celebration. It was really beautiful, so beautiful, that I wish we all could have been there.

Eugen Lewin-Dorsch

The Fairy Tale about the Wise Man

(1923)

 nce upon a time there was a wise man who studied books his entire life, and that was all he did. He wore gray steel-rimmed glasses, which was known to be a sign of great learning. Everything appeared gray to him as though made out of thick and misty fog, and he considered that to be the way things should be.

"Everything can be taken for anything else," he used to say if he happened by chance to look at the world. Indeed, he did that very seldom because he did not think it worth the effort. However, books were a different matter altogether. He thought they were the most important things in the world because one could learn everything there was to know from them, and every day he went to a bookshop to buy a new book. And even though the way to the bookshop led through short and quiet streets, it always seemed to him as though he were on an important and difficult mission, as though the king himself had summoned the wise man to explain something. On the return trip he held the new book carefully in his hand as though it were a precious gift. He regarded it lovingly and tenderly as though he himself had not only conceived it but had also written it, printed it, and, last but not least, had even bound the spine with decorative and solid leather and linen. Yes, that was how things were. And the people who encountered the wise man on the street shook their heads in surprise and smiled. However, he didn't notice because he was so absorbed by his deep thoughts.

It was only with great effort that he would ultimately

Eugen Lewin-Dorsch, *Die Dollarmännchen* (Berlin: Malik Verlag, 1923). Illustrator: Heinrich M. Davringhausen. Tale: "The Fairy Tale about the Wise Man."

reach his room again, for he had to climb narrow winding stairs, four stories high, until he ended up underneath the roof. During the climb he would sigh from exhaustion and pause a moment on each landing to catch his breath, for he lived near heaven, which was only appropriate for a wise man. However, his home was a dreadful little room! A bed, a chair, a desk—I think that was all that was in the room except for the books. Poor as a churchmouse he was, and poor as a churchmouse he remained. And that was because he wouldn't allow anything in the world to disturb his thoughts.

Yet he did own something precious. And that was—you will hardly believe this—the gray steel-rimmed glasses that sat on his nose. The circumstances behind all of this were rather peculiar, and that's just the story I want to tell you now.

I

One beautiful evening many years ago, it had become pitch black outside, and a cold autumn rain was pounding heavily on the ground. As was his custom, the wise man sat at his desk and read by oil lamp in a thick old manuscript bound in pigskin. All of the secret and strange arts of the world-famous magician Katschekitakehi were written down in this ancient book, and on one page his picture was displayed in a pretty, fine woodprint just as he was supposed to have looked in reality. The wise man read and read until his eyes became bleary and red and the letters began dancing back and forth before him as though they were keeping time to a merry waltz.

"My eyes are getting weak from all of this studying," he murmured to himself. "I think I need glasses." Just at that moment there was a knock on the door; indeed, there were three knocks, one after the other.

"Come in," he called out, somewhat irritated, for he didn't like to be disturbed while reading under any circumstances. "Come in!"

Slowly the door opened, and an old, strange-looking large man entered the room. He was wearing a large cone-shaped cap made out of paper on his head, and it was decorated and colored with weird symbols. His long white beard touched his shoes and was tied in a thick knot so that it would not have to sweep along the floor. A black wooden box hung around his neck attached to a leather string, the kind that door-to-door salesmen sometimes carry, and in his right hand he held a cane that was almost as long as he himself was tall. On top of the cane was a golden knob that sparkled like a candle flame. And the thing that was especially astonishing was that the man was completely dry from the top of his cone-shaped cap to the bottom of his beard, even though it was pouring cats and dogs outside, and he didn't even have an umbrella with him. But the strangest thing was yet to come.

The wise man looked up from his book, and suddenly his face became paralyzed with horror and fright. Why? Well, he was sure that he was staring straight at the magician whose very picture he had just been studying so carefully in the book. Wasn't it really the man in person?

"Good evening, professor!" the man with the cone-shaped cap said. "Excuse me for disturbing you so late. It's true. We do know each other. In truth, I'm the world-famous magician Katschekitakehi, whom you've been reading about in the book, and I'm coming directly from page three hundred seventy-six."

"My respects," the wise man stuttered in embarrassment. "My respects!" (He couldn't find the appropriate thing to say right at that moment, as is often the case with wise men.) And he bowed three times in a row almost scraping the ground. "How may I be of service to you?"

"I'd like to perform some magic here," Katschekitakehi answered, and at the same time he opened his box and drew forth three pairs of glasses. "I have here three pairs of magic glasses, and I want to give you one pair as a gift. If you choose the glasses with the yellow tint, then you will become the richest man in the world and will possess immense treasures of gold and jewels. If you choose the red glasses instead, you will marry a pretty princess and will always be happy and merry. However, if you select the gray glasses, you will become the wisest man in the world and will be able to understand each and every book that exists."

"That's wonderful!" the wise man exclaimed, clapping his hands in joy. He was as happy as a child. Without taking a long time to think about it, he grabbed the gray magic glasses.

But just at that moment there was a horrible explosion that terrified the wise man and knocked him to the ground, where he lay unconscious. The window popped open mysteriously. The wind hissed into the room like a cat and extinguished the oil lamp so that it became pitch black. Only the golden knob of the magician's cane still glowed in the darkness like burning phosphorus. And in this pale light one could see the strange figures and symbols suddenly rise up on the magician's cone-shaped paper cap and begin to move and dance up and down, playing all sorts of pranks.

Finally, the light faded as well, and the pages of the ancient book with the story about the magician Katschekitakehi began to flap. The noise sounded like the fluttering wings of a bird. Then suddenly everything was silent. After a while the wise man regained consciousness. But—a miracle!—he wasn't lying on the ground but was sitting straight in his chair. Katschekitakehi had disappeared without a trace. The window was closed. The oil lamp burned peacefully as though nothing at all had happened, and in front of the wise man was the thick old book.

"Was it all nothing but a dream?" he asked himself. He looked at the book, and page 376 lay open in front of him. The picture of the magician stood large as life before his eyes—the magician with the knotted beard, the cone-shaped cap, the cane, and the black box, all in a quiet and lovely woodprint. Yet the longer and more carefully he studied the picture, the more it seemed to him that the eyes of the magician rolled in a weird way and winked at him mockingly while everything else stood still. It seemed to him as though the strange figures on the cone-shaped cap began to transform themselves in a mysterious way.

"Did I really dream?" he asked himself, and he grasped his forehead with his hands in order to concentrate as he thought. What was that? There were glasses on his nose! Quickly he looked into a mirror, and indeed, he wore large gray steel-rimmed glasses. His astonishment became even greater when he tried to take them off and realized that they were glued firmly to his nose. Even when he sought to move them, they wouldn't budge. Then he knew for certain that he was wearing the magic glasses that were given to him by the world famous magician Katschekitakehi.

II

From that day onward the wise man became even wiser. His wisdom sprouted more quickly than a mushroom in autumn rain. From then on he could observe the world only through his glasses, and that is why things appeared to him in a totally different light. In fact, they seemed to dissolve and become one great gray mass. Everything had the same shade, just like shadows. It wasn't worth the effort to distinguish things in the world anymore.

That is why he began to absorb himself in his books all the more. He read and read and never tired of reading, from early morning until late at night. The walls of his small room were covered with books. They were also scattered on the floor and formed hills and mountains over which he had to climb like a mountain climber if he wanted to move around his room. But he rarely moved, only in exceptional situations. And thus he gradually became the wisest man in the world.

You can probably imagine that such immense reading had a particularly large influence on the wise man's nose. Indeed, there was a great change that came over the nose, and that was not unusual. After all, it was the nose that carried the magic glasses. My God, how serious, how learned, how contemplative that nose became and how distinguished from other noses. That is just as it should be for the nose of a wise person. Yes indeed, it thought highly of itself, and it carried the glasses with great dignity and respectability. When the wise man sat at his desk, bent over his books, he gave the impression that he was reading with his nose, not with his eyes, such was the seriousness and zeal with which the nose followed the numerous letters on the page. In time it actually grew long and sharp because of all of that work. It pecked, so to say, the golden kernels of wisdom, which were strewn on the pages of the books.

In front of the house in which the wise man lived, there was a stately linden tree, and its top faced his window. Every day at noon a small, lively sparrow came and sunned itself there and looked curiously into his room. Thus, it noticed the long sharp nose moving itself back and forth between the pages of the books.

"What can that be?" the bird asked himself. And since, as bird, he was accustomed to seeing something birdlike in all things on this earth, he imagined that the wise man's head bent over the book was a hen and that his smart nose was its beak. Of course, the gray steel-rimmed glasses appeared to him as a symbol of special bird superiority. The sparrow was a very talkative creature and loved to spend cozy hours chatting in the warm afternoon sun. One beautiful afternoon, when the rays of the sun shone with particular warmth and fondness on the top of the linden tree, the sparrow gathered up courage, puffed himself up mightily to make a distinguished appearance, and then called out to the reading head with a cheerful "Peep! Peep!" That was the polite and graceful way he introduced himself to his neighbor.

"I've recently moved here and live underneath the roof just a few steps away," he said, "and I'd be very happy to make friends with such an excellent and venerable bird!" He used the familiar form of address while speaking to the head, which he mistook for a hen, because it is customary among birds to be familiar with one another. Naturally, the wise man didn't understand one word the sparrow spoke because there has never been a book published on bird language up to the present. Yet the loud chirping did disturb his concentration. So he got up, climbed over the mountains of books, and closed the window. Of course, the sparrow flew away as quickly as possible when he realized to his horror that he had been talking to a man. And all of this misunderstanding was largely because of the nose.

Despite all of this, the sparrow sat on the linden tree the very next day and basked in the golden sunshine. Indeed, the sparrow had become very curious, and moreover, there was no treetop in the entire neighborhood as tall and as beautiful as that one. So he sat on his branch as still as a mouse. He didn't dare utter a "peep." Instead, he leaned over a little and looked at the head of the wise man, at his nose, at the gray steel-rimmed glasses, and the open book. Naturally, he didn't understand one thing about the entire affair.

III

Years passed, and the wise man became old and gray. And he could not become any wiser than he had already become, even with the best of will. One dreary fall evening, the rain poured in buckets from heaven, and the wind howled through the streets as though it wanted to turn them inside out. The wise man sat at his desk and read by the light of the oil lamp. He was coming to the end of the book, and as he read the last page, he clapped the book closed with a loud noise and said to himself in a ceremonious tone, "I've now read all of the books there are to read. So I'm going to write a book myself about the essence of the world."

He had barely spoken those words when a tumultuous thunder sounded and shook all of the corners and walls of the room. The oil lamp went out, and it suddenly became as dark as night. The huge number of books lying on the floor stampeded like a wild herd of sheep frightened by a storm. The large manuscripts sprang from their bookcases as if they had been terrified. The ancient book that contained the strange story about the magician Katschekitakehi fell right on to the desk in such a way that it opened to page 376 and revealed the woodcut, with the magician himself gazing from the page.

All of this lasted but a few seconds. However, who can describe the astonishment of the wise man when Katschekitakehi stood in person right before his very eyes. He held in his hand his long cane that was topped by a golden knob which glowed dimly in the room. His head was covered by the paper cone-shaped cap, and his silver white beard grazed the floor with its knot. The figures on the pointed cap danced back and forth like mad, and it seemed to the wise man as if they were sticking out their tongues and making faces at him.

"Good evening, professor!" the magician said. "How are you?"

"Just fine, great master," replied the old man. "Your magic glasses made me into the wisest of all men, and I owe you my gratitude."

"Don't mention it! I've come here once again to do a little more magic. As I've just learned, you have finished reading all of the books there are to read, and you want to write one yourself."

"Naturally, with your help, most famous Katschekita-kehi," the wise man stuttered in embarrassment.

"This is an excellent idea," the magician continued. "To do this, however, you need much better glasses than you have." With these words he opened his black box and took out steel-rimmed glasses as black as coal.

"Here they are." He stretched out his hand, took the gray glasses from the nose of the wise man and replaced them with the black ones. Right at that moment the wise man felt a pain in his nose, for the black glasses became fastened to his nose immediately, and the nose itself grew somewhat longer and sharper. It looked almost like a pencil.

"What do you see now?" the magician asked.

"Nothing at all," the wise man answered, for that was really the case.

"Then that's just right," Katschekitakehi said. "You can now recognize the essence of the world. Farewell."

Again there was some tumultuous thunder. The glow from the knob of the magician's cane went out. The pages of the ancient book that contained the life and works of the world-famous magician Katschekitakehi flapped loudly, and right then the magician disappeared as suddenly as he had come. However, the wise man had become unconscious again on his chair. When he regained consciousness, the oil lamp was burning peacefully on the desk as if nothing at all had happened, and page 376, with the picture of the magician, lay open in front of him. But he couldn't see the illustration because the black magic glasses were sitting on his nose. The only thing he could do was to write. His hands felt for a thick book with writing paper in his desk drawer, and he took out some paper. Then he moved a large ink bottle in front of him, dipped a feather pen into the ink, and began writing large beautiful letters on top of the first page: "The Essence of the World."

Of course, this was pure philosophy. And, if I were to

try to explain to you all that the wise man wrote down in his book, you would have the same feeling that the little sparrow had as he sat and watched from his sunny tree-top. You wouldn't understand a thing, and you'd only say "peep" to it all.

"Peep!" the sparrow said, in truth, but he didn't say it just once; he repeated himself at least a hundred times. And he didn't say it alone, for he had married a lovely sparrow, pretty as a picture, at the beginning of spring. Now both of them sat close together on the branch, as is only appropriate for newlyweds, and they chirped one after the other, "Peep! Peep!" At times the sparrow tried to sing a song because he was so happy. Yet it is well known that even the measly chaffinch is a better artist than the sparrow. The sun beamed, and the new leaves of the linden tree sprouted and unfolded with brilliance in the light of spring. The sparrow puffed his feathers, feeling at ease with himself, and he told his wife about all of the wonders of the world—about tele-graph wires and how one could swing on them, about a nest of swallows under the gable roof where they wanted to move that day, about a rather remarkable garbage can in the neighbor's house, and especially about the fresh horse manure.

In the meantime the wise man wrote about the es-sence of the world. Sometimes the two sparrows looked with curiosity into his room. The feather pen moved con-stantly and rapidly over the white paper, and the nose carrying the black glasses followed it just as rapidly. By now the nose looked exactly like a pencil, long and sharp. It actually seemed as though the nose wrote down all the black marks. At any rate, the nose did as-sume a most serious air, and it paid close attention to make sure that everything was correct. The two curious sparrows looked at the black letters, but they had no idea at all what they meant—and of course, these letters had great meaning! Even if the sparrows had known this, they would not have been impressed in the least because they were newlyweds and crazy about horse manure.

"Perhaps they're flies and mosquitoes," the sparrow said.

"We've got to tell the swallow about this," his wife replied.

And they swooped down toward the street.

One evening the wise man dipped his feather pen in the ink bottle for the last time. He wrote the final words in his book about the essence of the world on the last page, and he inked a large dot after the final word.

"Now I'm finished!" he exclaimed, and he rubbed his hands in joy. "May the great magician Katschekitakehi be praised!"

Just then there was a tumultuous thunder for the last time. The oil lamp went out. The books danced and jumped on the floor as if they were possessed by a demon, and those on the bookshelves crashed to the floor and danced and jumped with the other books. And once gain, like the last time, the ancient book with the life and works of the magician Katschekitakehi fell upon the table, and once again—what do you think—the book opened to page 376, with the picture of the magician. All at once the magician himself stood in the middle of the room. This time the knob on his cane glowed as bright as a star, and the figures on the cone-shaped cap raced so wildly and chaotically, with terrible faces, that it seemed as though they were being paid to do that.

"Good evening, professor!" Katschekitakehi said. "Today I'm going to perform some magic for the last time." And with that he laughed so loudly and horribly that he sent shivers up the spine of the wise man. Then the magician swung his cane three times through the air and cried out, "Hocus, pocus, fidibus!" He hit the wise man on the forehead with the golden knob, so hard that the man disappeared on the spot without leaving a trace behind. It was as if he had been blown away! Yes, yes, it all seems impossible. And at the same time the pages in the book about the essence of the world flapped loudly back and forth.

But to tell the truth (for lying wouldn't help me at all), the wise man did not completely disappear without a trace. Instead, the world-famous magician Katscheki-takehi used his magic to transport the wise man into the very book he wrote. And there he was on page 1 of *The Essence of the World*, portrayed in a pretty and artistic woodcut. He looked exactly as he had last looked: the long sharp nose was there, and the wise man held a thick book in his hands.

Katschekitakehi sat down by himself at the desk. He took the wise man's book in his hands, studied the woodcut that he had created with magic, and contemplated it in the glow of his golden knob. Then he grasped the feather pen and wrote underneath: "The wisest man in the world, author of this book, depicted true to life by the world-famous magician Katschekitakehi." Then he rapped the ancient book containing an account of his life and works with his cane, and he used magic to transport himself in a flash back onto page 376, from which he had come.

Since now there was nobody left in the room except the numerous books—the two woodcuts remained silent in their books without moving—I have nothing more to tell, and this story is finished.

At most I could perhaps say something more about the sparrows and how they looked into the room the next day from the top of the linden tree. The sun shone again, and they were astonished that nobody was there. "Peep!" said the sparrow, and "Peep!" answered his wife. And from this we can gather that they were in complete agreement on this point. Since everything remained quiet, they fluttered over to the window sill, and from there they moved to the desk and finally to the book about the essence of the world, which they began pecking with their beaks.

"It's not alive!" the sparrow said and hopped cheerfully over the pages.

"We could use this for our nest," his wife declared, and then they both began to tear the paper into shreds to build walls for their new nest.

And with this our story has now really come to an end.

Kings, Tyrants, Misers, and Other Fools

Maria Szucisch

The Holy Wetness
(1924)

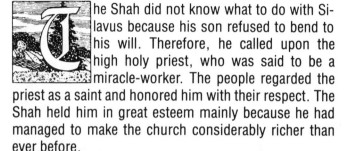he Shah did not know what to do with Silavus because his son refused to bend to his will. Therefore, he called upon the high holy priest, who was said to be a miracle-worker. The people regarded the priest as a saint and honored him with their respect. The Shah held him in great esteem mainly because he had managed to make the church considerably richer than ever before.

"Just think of it," the Shah said to the high priest, "my son would sooner deny me than abandon the common people. Come to my palace and convert him."

The high priest went to the palace of the Shah and spoke to Silavus, "I shall save your lost soul."

However, Silavus replied, "Allow me first to tell you a story."

And he told the story about "The Holy Wetness."

Once upon a time there was a dervish who would have liked to become high priest in the court of the Shah because that would have brought him great comfort and prestige. However, he knew nobody of influence to recommend him to the Shah.

I must win the favor of the people, he thought; if the Shah sees that I possess power over the people, then he will grant me the honor of becoming the high priest on his own impulse.

So he went into the desert and looked for a bare mountain cliff. After he found the cliff and was certain that he could stand on it comfortably, he returned to the city and looked for a plain, simple woman. And he said

Maria Szucisch, *Silavus,* translated by Stefan J. Klein
(Berlin: Malik, 1924). Illustrator: Otto Schmalhausen.
Cover art.

to the woman, "Follow me, my angel, and love me. If you remain faithful to me, I shall never forget you. I shall reward your work and loyalty with riches."

The woman followed the dervish into the desert. From then on, the dervish stood on the cliff from early morning until late evening for many years while the woman rode on a mule into the city and worked hard to earn a living for the two of them.

Caravans traveled through the desert, and the people noticed the dervish standing on the cliff and offered him food and drink. However, he refused their offerings and said, "I don't drink or eat, for the Lord has chosen me as one of his saints."

Since they did not see anyone who could have given him food or drink, they believed what the man said. They kissed the rocks on which he stood and carried the news about this miracle to distant lands.

However, things did not happen the way the dervish had hoped.

The news about his holiness was circulated for naught throughout the land, and the people made pilgrimages to him without his benefitting from them, for the Shah did not travel to the desert to make him his holy priest.

One day as the woman was about to ride her mule into the city again, the dervish said to her, "My true flower, when you arrive in the city, go to the palace of the Shah and shout: 'There is a high cliff tall as a tower in the desert. A dervish is standing on the cliff, and he leads a holy life. He refuses to sleep with a woman, to eat, or to drink. In spite of this, he's still alive. Let him become our high priest, for he is a saint.' But make sure you shout this three times."

When the woman arrived in the city, she stood in front of the Shah's palace and shouted loudly as the dervish had commanded. At first nobody paid attention to the woman. However, as she cried out for the third time, there were many onlookers who also began to shout, "There is a high cliff tall as a tower in the desert. A dervish is standing on the cliff, and he leads a holy life. He refuses to sleep with a woman, to eat, or drink. In spite of this, he's still alive. Let him become our high priest, for he is a saint."

Each time this was shouted, the number of people increased. When the Shah saw the crowd of people in front of the palace, he did not ask whether the report about the dervish was true or false. Instead, he assembled his splendid household and made his way into the desert. Upon finding the dervish, he showed him great respect and said, "When I find it necessary, the will of the people is sometimes sacred, and thus I want you to become the high priest at my court."

The dervish followed the Shah, but the woman remained in the desert. She waited for the appropriate time when the high priest would send for her since he owed his high position to her efforts. But the dervish did nothing. So the woman took the five children whom she and the dervish had produced over the course of years, and she made her way with them to the high priest, who at that very moment was being entertained in great splendor by the Shah. The woman threw herself at the feet of the Shah and lamented: "Lord, what shall become of me and my children. The high priest promised me a rich reward for my faithfulness and work, and behold he has given me nothing of the kind."

The high priest replied with great authority, "Go to the devil, you crazy person! Seek your justice in hell! You yourself proclaimed that I had never slept with a woman. How could you have had children with me? The evil spirits of hell want you to slander me so that you may help them darken my magnificence!"

Everyone agreed that the high priest was right, and the woman barely managed to escape a hard beating.

Realizing that she had sought justice in vain, and realizing that she had worked in vain for the deceitful and flattering dervish, she took her children and began searching for hell. She searched and searched until she found it. When the king of the devils heard her complaint, he was astonished. "The high priest has deceived you again," he said. "He knows for sure that I cannot bring about justice for good people like you. Go to God. This is his affair."

And so the woman searched again until she found God. In despair, she pleaded her case: "Lord, let justice be done! Reward me and punish the high priest who has acted so mercilessly against me!"

When God learned about the cruelty of the high priest, he became furious. "I cannot allow the sin of the high priest to go unpunished," he said. "Stay here with your children. I shall think of a suitable punishment for the high priest."

God began to reflect: "How can I punish the high priest? I must find a punishment to suit his crime!"

That night he sent one of the dervish's children to earth and had him sleep in the bed of his father.

"This shall be my punishment!" God said.

The high priest slept so soundly that he did not even notice the small child lying in bed next to him. The night was cold. The small child got none of the blankets and froze the entire night.

Early in the morning God summoned the child to heaven again.

"I must try something else since the high priest slept so soundly that he didn't even notice the child at all."

A few hours later he looked down into the bedroom of the high priest again and saw that the priest's face was horrified, for he was staring at a wet sheet and wondering to himself: Who did this? And he quickly hid the sheet.

"Just look how easy it has been for the freezing child to punish his father," God thought, and from then on he sent one of the small children to the bed of the high priest each night. Since the children got none of the blankets, the high priest found the sheet wet every morning. He became more and more horrified, and each morning he hid the wet sheet. Then he noticed that the servants and subordinate priests were whispering behind his back.

"What are you whispering?" he asked.

"For some days now we've noticed that you've been taking away your bedsheet each morning and then hiding it. The servants never find a sheet in your bed."

Then the high priest said to his subordinates, "Come sleep in my bedroom, and see what happens to the sheet."

They did as the high priest commanded. When they had all taken their place on the carpet, the high priest blew out the oil lamp, took the blankets from the bed, and lay down next to the others. He did not dare sleep in bed because he was not sure what would happen.

Once again God sent a child to the bed of his father. Though the child found nobody in bed, he lay down, and because there were no blankets, he froze the entire night and wet the sheet again.

Early the next morning God summoned the child to him.

One of the subordinate priests was the first to awaken, and he was astonished to find that the high priest was lying next to the others on the ground and that the bedsheet was wet. He awakened the sleeping priests, pointed to the wet sheet, and asked, "Who could have done this?"

The high priest himself was astonished but spoke with authority to the others: "This wet bed is a holy wetness. It could only have come from a divine visitation!"

The news of this miracle spread rapidly in the city, especially since the high priest and his assistants circulated the report. The faithful came in droves to look at the holy wetness. The high priest had the wet spots of the sheet cut into tiny pieces, and anyone could acquire a piece if he paid a gold coin.

When God saw what had become of his punishment, he stopped sending the children to the bed of their father. Instead, he said, "Woman, I cannot punish the holy priest!"

And though God no longer sent the children to the bedroom, the holy wetness continued to appear.

The deceitful dervish is still holy priest. The holy wetness is inexhaustible, and for a gold coin anyone can buy a piece of the wet sheet.

"Here is where my story ends," Silavus said.

The high priest exclaimed, "I shall condemn you for making a mockery of my person!" And he wanted to take to his heels.

But Silavus blocked his way. "Tell me," he said, "what should the people do with a God who doesn't protect them? What should they do with a God who has no power to punish the sins of the rich?"

Robert Grötzsch

The Enchanted King
(1922)

his is the story about the king who became a cripple. In the past the soldiers used to talk a great deal about this event around campfires, and they all agreed that King Blackbeard had gotten what he deserved, for Blackbeard had been a vicious tyrant.

Indeed, he once ruled over a great people who were extremely unhappy because Blackbeard forced the country into one war after another. The neighboring countries feared him because they felt he might attack them at any moment, so great was his greed for the treasures of other countries! His own people hated him because he caused the men of his country to die on distant battlefields. The hordes of cripples grew continually, and the fields were being devastated by war. At one point, during a hunt in the woods, Blackbeard encountered a pious hermit whom he sentenced to hang because the man demanded that the king let his neighbors live in peace. In fact, there were men in the kingdom who said, "We must overthrow the king, or the country will collapse."

That was the way things were under Blackbeard's rule when an old troubadour happened to pass through the land followed by many people. He had a wavy beard and long white hair; he played a lute and sang about the evil King Blackbeard and his terrible deeds. So Blackbeard sent his guards to fetch him to the castle, where the king smiled grimly and then commanded, "Sing me the song that you bellow in the streets!"

Whereupon the troubadour sang the song in such a blunt manner that Blackbeard first turned pale and then red. And when the last stanza faded away, the king said to the troubadour, "Within the next hours your body will dangle miserably from the gallows!"

"In your next battle you will be thrown to the ground and lie there miserably," the troubadour answered calmly and hung the lute over his back.

"You are really bold, troubadour," Blackbeard scoffed and then stood up angrily on his throne. "For that you will now suffer for several weeks in a dungeon before I have you swing from the gallows!"

To this the troubadour replied, "You will hobble as cripple for more than a hundred years until death ends your suffering!"

Blackbeard laughed loudly and furiously. "The fool is crazy! Throw him into the darkest dungeon so he can come to his senses!"

However, when the king's bodyguards were about to grab the troubadour, he threw the men aside as though he possessed magic power. And when they tried to pursue him, he disappeared from sight. However, the guards at the gate and drawbridge swore that they saw a man with a wavy beard and flowing white hair fly by them on a lute through the air.

Blackbeard cursed angrily, stomped around the castle, had the guards thrown into prison, and then sent out a hundred knights who had to roam all over the land in search of the troubadour—in vain! The troubadour had disappeared.

Now Blackbeard began to brood. He was forced to think constantly about the gloomy prophecy of the old man. He couldn't figure it out, and the longer he thought about the mysterious words, the more he began to curse. The more he cursed, however, the more furious he became; and when Blackbeard could not control his anger, he generally started a new war.

That is what happened in this case too. Just three days after the troubadour had disappeared, Blackbeard called together the soldiers of his land and attacked the neighboring country—scorching, burning, and murdering everywhere. A bloody battle erupted that lasted from early morning until late in the evening. As the sun was setting and blood flowed in the trenches of the battlefield, a strange knight emerged in the middle of the tumult. Wearing a suit of shiny armor and a white helmet, he sat erect on a white stallion, and he swung a sword that sprang up and down like a hammer. Blackbeard's knights scattered as they saw this white knight advance, and before King Blackbeard could raise his blade, his lightning-quick enemy pounded the royal armor with strokes as if from a violent hailstorm. One blow sent the king's helmet flying, another slashed his arm, and a third went through Blackbeard's leg. He fell from his horse as if he were dead.

That was the end of Blackbeard's majestic glory, for when he opened his eyes that very same night, he had become a crippled little man—a man in the shape of a hunchback, with a lame leg and a crippled arm whose hand held a crutch. The battlefields around the little man were deadly silent, but right in front of him sat an old man with a wavy beard and long white hair glistening in the moonlight. Next to the old man there was a bright shiny coat of armor and a white helmet. Blackbeard's eyes popped wide open. "The troubadour—the white knight!" he muttered trembling, and he knew now that some sort of magician was sitting before him.

"You've guessed right," the old man replied. "I'm the troubadour and the white knight and even more, but you're no longer King Blackbeard. I've patched you together so that you will hobble around for more than a hundred years as a cripple, just as I predicted. You were the terror of your country and your neighbors and caused death for others thousands of times, and now you shall limp from battlefield to battlefield for this and suffer death thousands of times. The crutch will be your master and servant. It will propel you from place to place, and when you turn it, it will make you invisible. Whenever you come across a dying man, this piece of wood will also fulfill his last two wishes. You only need to stamp the crutch on the ground, and the wishes of the dying man will be fulfilled. And only when someone forgets the second wish after the first, then death will finally relieve your suffering while the other man shall live!"

With this, the old man drew an ivory wand from his gown, waved it over Blackbeard's head, and pointed to the west, from which a white stallion came trotting. The old man mounted the horse and then rode rapidly away. But Blackbeard felt an irresistible force urging him to move toward the open fields. So he stood up, propped himself with the crutch, and hobbled into the morning dawn.

From then on Blackbeard's existence was dreadful. Shriveled and crippled, shy and unsteady, he limped through fields and woods. Generally he avoided people, but wherever a war erupted, he was drawn there through inner force. If he hesitated, the crutch hit his leg until he made his way to the war. When death and night covered the battlefields, he came out of the woods. Wherever a dying soldier sighed, he had to kneel down, had to fulfill the last wishes of the gasping fighter, had to suffer through the death throes and pain of the soldier. As soon as the last two wishes were fulfilled, the wounded soldier would be relieved by death; but Blackbeard had to live on between blood and corpses, groans and death rattles.

He tried to put an end to his tormented life many times, but he had no power over his shriveled body. If he stabbed himself, his blood would not flow. If he tried to drown himself by jumping into the water, his crutch would carry him ashore. If he hung himself, the rope would break.

Entire generations of people died, and new ones were born. Old times went, and the new came, while war and peace took turns in the march of time. However, the crippled little man remained. The older he became, the more his body became shriveled and ugly. The more shaggy and wild his hair and beard became, the more the people were horrified when they encountered the small crippled man in the woods. If he was asked by someone what he was looking for, he would answer, "Salvation," and he would make himself invisible with the crutch and hobble away. Yet salvation did not come. None of the dying soldiers forgot the second wish after the first one. On the contrary, most of them wanted three wishes.

In the meantime three centuries passed. The crippled little man's crutch became decrepit, and the cripple often beseeched the trees of the woods to end his life. Once again bloody times were at hand. The little man was driven from one dying man to the next, and he experienced many deaths every day. A great horrendous war raged in Germany, where the Germans, French, Russians, Bashkirs, and Croatians fought against each other. They ravaged cities and villages, trampled the fields, and fought bloody, murderous battles.

One of these battles lasted three nights and three days. On the evening of the third day there were large stacks of dead soldiers covering the field, and hundreds of wounded men groaned as the sun set. A huge shadow covered part of the woods where a young bugler, who was seriously wounded, lay stretched out on the grass. He felt death in his chest and made a fist right at that moment because he thought of the enemy soldier who had knocked him from his horse and who had slashed his head and shoulder with a saber. It had been a red-headed French dragoon.

The wounded man passed his hand through his bloody blond hair and sighed as though he couldn't accept the fact that he would never see the sun again, never hunt on his horse, and never blow his bugle. Before all this had happened, he had led a carefree life and enjoyed wine and women. That is why it was now not so easy for him to die. He cursed the red-headed enemy, rolled over, and searched feverishly for his fine sword. And as he glanced over the grass, he gasped suddenly in horror. There, in front of him, leaning on a crutch—there stood a shriveled, ancient little man with a shaggy beard and wild hair.

"The cripple!" the bugler exclaimed, for he had often heard rumors about him from the soldiers around the campfires. They said that whenever the crippled appeared before a wounded man, it meant his death. That is why the bugler was no longer surprised when the little man began to talk. "Tonight you are about to die. If you have two wishes, tell them to me quickly!"

The bugler did not need much time to reflect. "If I must die now, then I'd like to blow the bugle one more time, and then"—he made two fists, and hate vibrated in his throat—"then I'd like to kill the red-headed dragoon who knocked me off my horse!"

He had hardly uttered the last word when the little crippled man stamped the ground with his crutch and a beautiful shiny bugle lay next to the cavalier. Hastily he grabbed the glittering instrument and looked at it with beaming eyes. Then he straightened himself up a little and began to blow. He played a beautiful old song about love, passion, happiness, and war. His wound no longer bothered him, and his chest burst with joy, for magic tones came out of the bugle, as pure as the sound of bells and as glorious as the music of angels.

And then something miraculous happened. The battlefield, which had lain silent in the evening light, became alive. The wounded men raised their heads, stood up, forgot their wounds and pain, and hobbled toward the bugle. They sat down in a semicircle around the bugler and listened to the song with rapt faces. They all came, friends and foes, Bavarians and Prussians, Pandorians and French, Bashkirs and Croatians. And even those men in the camps whose fires were blazing all around, friend and foe alike, joined the rest as if they never wanted to fight against one another again, as if they never wanted to have anything to do with war again. Many of them sat with feverish heads and bloodied bodies, but there was happiness and peace in all of their faces. The more people rushed to hear the bugle, the more beautiful the song became, and the bugler played even more splendidly. He blew until there was a camp of colorful uniforms all around him, an army of soldiers from different countries. He blew until he was out of breath.

It was only then that he stopped and listened to the music, which continued to float miraculously through the air as though it never wanted to vanish. And he regarded the colorful picture of peace that was right in front of him. His eyes glistened. He no longer knew anything about war and bloodshed and was unable to distinguish friend from foe. His wounds and pain were gone—with the exception of a light throb in his back. This came from the little crippled man.

"Hurry up! I've got to move on. I've got to go," the cripple muttered. He stamped with the crutch, and the bugle disappeared like lightning. In its place was a loaded pistol. "Shoot! There's the man who knocked you down." The little man raised his voice and pointed to a red-headed French dragoon who was squatting between two Prussian musketeers.

However, the bugler shook his head and refused to shoot. Indeed, he did recognize the dragoon, but he no longer knew why he should kill him. His hate had disappeared. So he threw the pistol as far as he could into the woods, looked at friends and foes who sat peacefully side by side as though war no longer existed, and lost in thought, he said, "If it could only remain this way. I have no other wish than this."

As the little crippled man heard this, he stared with green eyes: the bugler had forgotten the second wish after the first! The cripple's eyes became more and more starry. His breath became heavy, and he shrank with the crutch until he became nothing but a gray lump. In time the lump became a strange angular rock, which still stands today at the edge of those woods in the shape of a hunchbacked dwarf.

The bugler fell into a deep, deep sleep. Two days later, he awoke and felt completely refreshed and healthy.

Robert Grötzsch

Burufu the Magician

(1922)

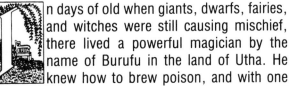n days of old when giants, dwarfs, fairies, and witches were still causing mischief, there lived a powerful magician by the name of Burufu in the land of Utha. He knew how to brew poison, and with one single word he could change friends into enemies and make happy people unhappy. Indeed, he delighted in anything that was evil, which is why the people of Utha were frightened of him. They avoided his company and called him the devil's grandfather.

"Pay me a tribute each year of one hundred cows and one hundred fields of wheat; then I won't harm you," Burufu declared to the people.

But the men of Utha shook their fists in outrage. "We're free men," they said. "We won't let ourselves be made into slaves! We'll chase the evil magician from the land! Away with the devil's grandfather!"

Burufu became furious and withdrew to his underground palace. Once he was there, he cursed and swore that he would exterminate the people. Nine days and nine nights he racked his brains to find the fastest way to wipe them out. On the tenth day he jumped up and said to himself, "Well, Burufu, they're not going to call you the devil's grandfather much longer. They're going to bash their heads against one another!" Upon saying this he hung some large kettles over the fire in his magic cellar, mixed various powders together, and let everything sizzle and simmer for three days. On the fourth day, he commanded: "Let the fire be gone!" Immediately the fire went out, and Burufu took from the kettle a clump that glittered like gold. He cast a spell on the clump, disguised himself as a wise man, went to the people, and threw the glistening clump into their midst.

"Oh, how wonderfully it glitters," the people said. They rejoiced and then began fighting over it.

"Yes, this is gold," Burufu explained. "It's the most precious thing that exists. And there is even more beneath the earth."

The people began to scrape and dig. They climbed down deep into the core of the earth and carried forth large amounts of gold. They quarreled over the precious stones. Everyone was envious of everyone else. Everyone wanted to have the most, and many people amassed treasures at home. They made enemies out of each other, and in fact, they attacked each other with weapons and murdered for the sake of gold.

Burufu, who watched all of this, laughed triumphantly and set upon his way to Mother White-Eyes, the old fortune-teller. He wanted her to tell him when the people would completely wipe themselves out.

Mother White-Eyes lived deep in the pathless woods and was so old that her eyes had become pale and yellow. They sat lifeless in their sockets. Yet she could see more with those blind eyes than others could whose eyes were alive and sparkling. When the old woman closed her lids and pressed her hands against her temples, she could see everything that was happening on the earth and everything that would happen on the earth in the future. It was to this fortune-teller that Burufu went, and he asked: "Mother White-Eyes, tell me what the people are doing now!

The old woman crouched on the ground, closed her eyes, and pressed her hands against her temples. Her face took on a terrible expression as she said, "Oh woe! An evil spirit has descended upon the people! Someone has spread gold in their midst. They are quarreling over it. They are murdering each other, and brothers are becoming each other's enemies because of the gold."

Robert Grötzsch, *Der Zauberer Burufu* (Berlin: Dietz, 1922). Illustrator unknown. Tale: "Burufu the Magician."

Burufu laughed with satisfaction. "Tell me more, Mother White-Eyes," he said. "What's to come?"

The old woman pressed her hands tightly against her temples and glimpsed the future of the people as the images flickered within her. "Oh, it looks bleak! The people will soon be divided into groups. Some will have a great deal of gold and others very little. Some will become masters, and others will be servants. Greed, envy, and lust for power will take hold of the people and will spread to other countries. And the people of different countries will start wars to obtain the gold of the others."

Burufu rejoiced. "Tell me more, Mother White-Eyes! When will the people wipe themselves out?"

Suddenly the old woman became angry. "You fool!" she scolded. "Human beings are not as weak as you think. Hundreds of thousands will die in wars for gold and wealth, but hundreds of thousands will be born again. And a great time will come when powerful iron machines will rumble, and a new spirit will inspire the people. Then they will all be honored according to their work. No longer will there be masters and slaves, and the people of different countries will live peacefully side by side. Then the spell you have cast on the gold, Burufu, will be broken, and the people will say: 'We've beaten the devil along with his grandfather!'"

Burufu leaped in the air as though he had been bitten by a snake. "To hell with the pack of idiots!" he yelled and cursed something terrible. Then he sped away and headed for his underground castle, where he locked himself in his magic kitchen and started a wild fire. "Burufu, whatever gold can't do, plague and sickness will finish," he said to console himself. He hung a large pot over the fire, poured poisonous liquids into it, and let everything brew for three days and three nights. On the fourth day he commanded: "Let the fire be gone!" The fire went out. Burufu filled three bottles with the contents of the poison potion and carried them to the people on a foggy night. He sneaked around and poured the

Robert Grötzsch, *Der Zauberer Burufu* (Berlin: Dietz, 1922). Illustrator unknown. Tale: "Burufu the Magician."

liquid of the first bottle into the rivers, ponds, and wells. He sprayed the liquid of the second bottle on the fruit and vegetables. He blew the liquid of the third bottle into the air. Then Burufu laughed and set upon his way to the fortune-teller.

"Mother White-Eyes, tell me what the people are doing now," Burufu demanded of the shriveled old woman. She crouched on the ground, closed her eyes, placed her hands against her forehead, and began: "Terrible! Horrible! A plague has crept from the wells and waters and is strangling the people one by one. The fruit and vegetables have been spoiled and are killing the people. Countless tiny germs are hovering in the air and are poisoning the people."

Burufu could hardly control himself. "More, Mother White-Eyes, more! When will all the people be dead and buried?"

The old woman looked straight at him and said angrily, "You fool! The people are smart creatures. Necessity will teach them how to fight against pestilence. Only the poor people who have suffered and been deprived because of the fight for gold—only the poor people will cry to no avail, and thousands of them will fall victim to disease. However, when the great time arrives, when the powerful machines begin to rumble, the poor people will group together and put an end to all kinds of tyranny. The people will work in bright airy rooms, and everyone will have enough to eat, and everyone will have enough time to relax in the country. Then all human beings will live healthier lives than they had ever lived before, and they will say: 'We drove away the devil along with his grandfather!'"

"Awful! Awful!" Burufu was furious and sped away again. He crawled into his underground palace, grumbled, and scolded himself: "Burufu, you old ass! Hey, Burufu, now you must make the worst poison of all. Something that tastes so good that the people will tear their hair out to get it, something that will be the end of them all. Do you understand, Burufu?" And once again he mixed, cooked, and brewed liquids in large pots for three days. Bubbles rose in the form of his brew, and when the bubbles burst, small invisible devils were hatched, and they cloaked themselves in foaming pearls and swam around in the brew. On the fourth day Burufu said, "Let the fire be gone!" The fire went out. Burufu filled many bottles with the contents of the pots. He put some of them into a pack and went to the people disguised as a merchant and let them taste the potion.

And each person who drank the liquid became cheerful, and gradually people swaggered down the street after Burufu bellowing, "One more drop, my dear man, just one more drop!" Burufu laughed and showed the people how to prepare the inebriating drink. The people listened carefully and then eagerly began their work. Again Burufu rushed to the blind fortune-teller and burst with joy about his new triumph.

"Now, Mother White Eyes, tell me what the people are doing now," he said in a good mood.

The old woman did what she always did. She crouched on the ground, pressed her hands against her forehead, shook her head sadly, and said, "Oh, the people have been blinded! In their misery they're now brewing intoxicating drinks and are pouring the stuff down their throats from cups and glasses. They don't realize that they're absorbing small foaming devils in their bodies with each drop they drink. The devils rise to their heads, confuse their minds, and suck the strength from their bodies!"

"Great!" Burufu muttered with satisfaction to himself. Then he added hastily, "More, Mother White-Eyes, more! When will the people drink themselves into the ground?"

The old woman stood up in irritation. "You fool!" she sneered. She stared ahead, and again the image of the future flickered before her eyes. "The people are indestructible creatures. They will drink down the intoxicating devils by the bucket. The wise people will warn the others in vain about the intoxicating poison. But the rich will not be disturbed in their drinking, for the devils will help them wile away the time. The poor people will drink to forget their poverty. Yet when the great time arrives, when the powerful machines rumble, and gold no longer divides the people, then they will smash the bottles containing the intoxicating poison. Human beings will live more happily than ever before, and they will say: 'The devil along with his grandfather is dead!'"

This time Burufu did not say one word. He stamped wildly with his feet and rushed madly to his underground palace, where he crawled to the deepest chamber and sighed. "Burufu, Burufu! Even your most brilliant ideas are ruined!" And he heard the words of the fortune-teller ringing continually in his ears: "A great time will come . . ." Oh how he hated it, this great time, when the people were to triumph despite his tricks! He, the great Burufu, was to be conquered, driven away, killed? A grim helpless feeling filled his heart, and he could neither relax nor sleep. Then, in his wretched condition, he thought about the intoxicating drinks, and in desperation he grabbed the bottles that he had filled when he made the last poison potions, and he drank as much as his stomach could hold. The devils in the bottle whisked into Burufu's skull, drove away all of his thoughts, and forced his head to slump to his chest in sleep. When Burufu awoke the next day, the grim helplessness burdened his heart even more strongly than before. So Burufu brewed a new large kettle filled with intoxicating liquor and drank himself to sleep and oblivion again.

Thus, he began doing this day-in, day-out, and the strong, fierce Burufu became a shaky fellow with a deformed stomach, gaunt face, drooping eyes, bluish-red nose, and bad breath. Whenever he looked at himself in the mirror, he became horrified by his reflection. And whenever he considered what had led to his decrepit condition, he hated the people even more passionately than before; he would think once again of ways to wipe them out. However, his brain had been completely devastated by the foaming little devils. What the smart Burufu had once tried to accomplish now became impossible for the drunkard Burufu. He ground his teeth and would have liked to quit drinking, but the little bottled evils had gained power over him and made him into an imbecile. "Drink! Drink!" they commanded and crawled into Burufu's arms and hands so that they trembled. And they danced until Burufu grabbed a bottle and drank. He would have liked to free himself from the invisible tyrants by using a magic spell, but the little devils had scared all of the magic spells out of his brain. The only thing he could still do was grind his teeth, curse, drink, and mix and brew strange alcoholic drinks in which the foaming little devils swam around.

One day when the drunken Burufu was hanging another kettle over the fire, the flames became so powerful that he wasn't able to control them. He would have liked to speak that magic spell with which he usually banished the dangerous fire, but the little devils had made the head of the magician so sluggish and numb that his tongue could only trill "Fi-fi-fire." Since he could no longer remember the magic words, the flames mounted. The flood in the kettle hissed, simmered, and boiled over. Burufu stammered, stuttered, and could think of nothing better to do in his imbecilic fright than to drink from the last bottles until they were empty. He drank so hastily that the hundreds of hundreds of little devils in his body foamed, swelled, and spewed bad fumes from his mouth. These fumes added oil to the fire, and there was an explosion. Burufu was on fire inside and outside and flew into the air.

The heat in the magic kitchen became a glowing and raging ocean. Sticky gases rose from the boiling kettle and burst into towering flames, which crackled so loudly that the ground quaked throughout the area, and the earth was sent soaring into the air and eventually formed a mountain. From the peak of the mountain the flames reached out to light the sky. So ended the life of the evil magician Burufu. His castle burned to cinders, and in its place a volcano arose from the ground and can still be seen today.

Oskar Maria Graf

Baberlababb

(1927)

nce upon a time in the valley of the mountain there was a teacher who frightened all of the children in the village school. He was quick to use the rod when someone made a mistake, and he never believed an excuse, whether it was true or false. He was as tall and lean as a tree. His mustache was twisted, and he was always in a grouchy mood. There was a rumor spread by those who knew him that he would go into the cellar whenever he laughed just so that nobody would see him.

If a child came late to school, if parents sent a letter of excuse with a child who had been sick, or if a pupil apologized for a mistake—nothing would help. The mean teacher would dismiss everything with a swift motion of his hand, and then he would bark grimly, "Baberlababb, Baberlababb, that's no reason!"

Many children came to the school from the surrounding valleys, from desolate places in the region, and from cabins that stood high on the slopes of the mountains. Poor people lived in those cabins. During the day they worked in the weaving factory or in the sawmill down in the village. There was always snow up there where they lived. Even in warm weather nothing grew on those rocky mountains that towered over the valley and displayed steep, ragged peaks. The people from the valley never climbed the slopes. At most a foolish mountain climber would sometimes lose his way and would be glimpsed on a slope crying for help. Every now and then one could see an eagle circling and threatening in the gray skies or mountain goats racing rapidly and gracefully over the rocks. That was all.

Early in the morning, when it was still dark, the people of the mountain cabins trotted through the snow down into the valley. They plowed a way for the children who would come later. And if it had snowed a great deal, they stuck branches into the ground from time to time to show the way.

"You've got to be careful, children, and follow the signs we leave behind," the parents would tell their young ones the evening before, and they generally did as they were told. However, one time it snowed so hard that the children could see neither their parents' tracks nor the planted branches, and they came to school very late. Anxiously they slipped through the door, but the teacher grabbed one after the other and beat them all.

"We couldn't find the path, teacher! It was completely covered with snow!" The children whimpered, but it was no use.

"Baberlababb! Baberlababb! That's no reason!" the angry teacher shouted and continued to beat them.

That evening, when the children returned home, they told their parents to plant larger branches. "We couldn't find the path and arrived late at school. So the teacher beat us."

And the men stuck much larger branches along the path. But it snowed and snowed, and when the children wandered toward the valley the next morning, they saw nothing but snow, and with each step they took, they sank deep into the drifts. They had managed to get halfway to the valley when they heard the church clock strike nine o'clock in the distance. Then they all lost heart, fell exhaustedly on the soft snow, and wept bitterly.

"Oh, if only someone would help us! If only someone would come!" they moaned desperately and looked around for help. Their gazes stretched first over the white spaces of snow and then into the endless gray sky teeming with flakes of snow. They were sweating because they had exerted themselves so much, and their clothes were damp from head to toe. They trembled from the frost and fear. They didn't know what to do anymore, and a boy by the name of Hans said glumly, "It's better to freeze here than to be beaten again. The teacher doesn't believe a word we say!" And they all nodded their heads exhaustedly and groaned. "What should we do now! If only someone would help us!"

All of a sudden—nobody knew how it happened—a huge, pure white spirit shot up from their midst and cried out, "Children, come with me!" And the voice was so friendly that the children followed him without fear. The white spirit marched onward, leaving wide tracks as he shoveled the snow away with his powerful feet. He plowed a path down into the valley, and the children descended. Once down in the village, the spirit disappeared. The children stood still for a few minutes staring and searching with their eyes. Then they ran to school.

No sooner had they opened the school door than the teacher rushed at them with his swinging rod.

"Teacher, teacher, something miraculous happened to us!" they exclaimed. "A snow spirit guided us to the village. Otherwise we would have frozen and been lost forever!" The children talked continually even though the teacher beat them. They told him all about their miraculous experience.

"Yes! Yes! A snow spirit!" Hans exclaimed and stood up like a man before the teacher. "We're not lying, teacher! A good snow spirit saved us. All of a sudden he came out of the ground and paved a way for us so we could come down from the mountain. Otherwise we would have frozen."

After Hans told the teacher this story without flinching, the teacher paused and deliberated a moment as though he were considering something. But then he became irritated again, and he shook his head brusquely.

"Baberlababb! Baberlababb! There's no such thing!"

he yelled at the boy all at once and shoved him to his desk. However, as he turned around, the powerful snow spirit suddenly stood in front of him and thundered at him, "There is such a thing! Come to the slope of the mountain tomorrow, and you will see for yourself!"

And quick as a wink, before the teacher could look up, the spirit was gone. Most of the children stood up and looked with horror at the spot where the strange phantom had stood. Only the mountain children sat at their desks. They were not afraid.

The teacher looked at them in a threatening way. He was furious. "Baberlababb! Baberlababb! There's no such thing!" he yelled. "Just wait. I'll look at everything more closely tomorrow, and then you'll get it!"

And indeed, he did climb the mountain early the next day. He made his way through the deep snow until he came to the edge of the mountain. It had not been snowing so hard when he had left the village, but all of a sudden the flakes of snow were so thick that he could see nothing around him. He heard only the voices of the mountain children, who were nearby, and after a while they were right next to him. They greeted him shyly and wanted to move on. However, now the snow had become so deep that even the teacher could not see over it; and despite all of his attempts with his arms and legs, he could not advance. He became somewhat discouraged, and even the children didn't know what to do. And then—in the wink of an eye—the snow spirit stood there again. He was just as friendly to the children as the day before, and he said, "Go straight ahead. The path is already plowed for you." And turning to the teacher, he said, "And you, teacher, just follow me nicely!" And down the mountain they went. The children marched merrily ahead. The spirit had really plowed an easy way. Nobody had seen him except the children.

The teacher wanted to follow, but the spirit constantly kicked the snow up into the air with his feet at each step as if he had never learned anything but this. The snow became so high and firm and impenetrable that the teacher could not advance anymore, and all at once he began to shout and complain, "In God's name, help! Help me, children, help!" The teacher yelled, pleaded, and fluttered about with his arms in the deep snow. He shouted and shouted: "I can't move anymore. Help, help!"

And at that moment the powerful snow spirit turned and thundered at him: "Baberlababb! Baberlababb! That's no reason!"

And the teacher could no longer hear the voices of the children. He saw nothing more of the spirit. Just snow and snow and more snow surrounded him. Then he disappeared.

In the spring, when the snow melted, he was still not to be found. Since then the children have had no trouble reaching the valley, and there is a good, friendly teacher in the school, where they are learning a great deal.

Whenever it snows in the winter, the mountain children only have to call out "Baberlababb," and then the vanished teacher emerges from the snow, silent and white, and he must pave a way for them toward the valley. And then he is swallowed by the snow again. And for many, many years now, that is the way things have been . . .

Oskar Maria Graf

The Fairy Tale about the King
(1927)

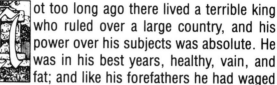 ot too long ago there lived a terrible king
who ruled over a large country, and his
power over his subjects was absolute. He
was in his best years, healthy, vain, and
fat; and like his forefathers he had waged
many wars, so his power grew greater and greater. He
had sent monstrous armies against peaceful neighbors
and caused widespread destruction. Countless numbers
of people lost their lives because of him. Yet he continued to act like a god and ruled as he pleased. Everyone
trembled before him; nobody dared to refuse his slight-
est wish. Thousands upon thousands of people worked
for him, and actually there was nothing for him to do
except indulge his moods. Because he became bored so
quickly, he had his fawning servants tell him stories
about his ministers and marshals. And when it pleased
him, when he became suspicious of one of his trusted
assistants after hearing some kind of story, he ordered
the person concerned to report to him. Then he would
make that person look ridiculous, mocking and insulting
him so much that the minister or marshal would request
to be dismissed from his office. Yet no sooner would the
minister or marshal express that wish than the king
would become extremely furious. He would take his
whip and lash the man to his heart's content. Then he
would have him thrown into prison.

And everyone obeyed the king. Everyone despised the
person who was to be punished.

But after this treatment had continued for years, after
more and more people displeased the king, after he took
out his wanton moods on his most trusted officers in

127

more and more disastrous ways, fear spread throughout the land. Nobody wanted to serve the king anymore. Everyone avoided him. They all sneaked away. They left the country and lived in foreign lands under assumed names. The situation became so grave that the king finally had to resort to choosing his trusted officials from the poor people.

One day he chanced to meet a sick old man and ordered him to be his chancellor. The old man, however, was stubborn; he refused. Despite all of the king's threats, he shook his head continually, until the king became so furious that he shot the toothless man in the throat just as the old man was about to open his mouth. There was a terrible cry, and then the old man sank to the ground dead.

The news of this dreadful deed spread through the capital as swiftly as the wind, and everyone fled from the tyrant. When the king left his residence to search once again for another chancellor, he found all of the streets and houses empty. His curses echoed in the bleak darkness. Nobody answered anymore. Upon his return to his castle, he found that even his servants had disappeared. Only his wife was left, alone, trembling, and pale. She sat on a golden cushioned chair and wept. The king was alone, too, for his wife sat next to him like a zombie.

Soon the king mounted his horse in anger and rode out into the wide, dark land to look for new ministers. But the refugees from the capital had long since spread the news about the king, and throughout the country there was great dread. Wherever the king went, the people bowed like dogs and said, "Yes, yes indeed, Your Majesty!" Yet the king would barely have moved out of sight before they would flee. Everywhere he went, the people scraped the dust of the ground as they bowed to the king. They smiled and pretended to be joyful or serious depending on the wishes of the king. Everywhere the people said, "Yes! Yes, indeed, Your Majesty!" And each time, after the tyrant had left the city, they breathed a sigh of relief. They embraced each other and felt that they had been saved. "Thank God, we're rid of him!" they exclaimed. "But now we must leave! Quick!"

And the king arrived in another city and announced harshly to the mayor and the city councillors, "I see that all of your people are disloyal to me. They shall be punished! They must bleed for their betrayal! I want war! The people are all to go to war! Announce this! This is my command! When I come again, I want to see the entire city turned into an armed camp!"

That was what he declared, and his voice roared like thunder in the large city hall. The walls trembled. None of the councillors dared to lift their bowed heads. They all feared for their lives and mumbled docilely, "Yes, your majesty. Yes indeed, Your Majesty!"

And the king rode onward.

On the evening of the same day there were posters in the entire city that proclaimed the will of the king. Everyone read the command and trembled. The rich people were horrified. They climbed into their cars, drove to doctors, and offered them great sums of money for a certificate declaring them unfit to serve in the army. Some shrewd people took to their beds and pretended to be sick. Others went to hospitals and had an operation just so they would not have to go to war. Many people took to flight with all of their possessions. Those people who remained hid their money and valuables and buried their jewels.

In the end the famished poor people were the only ones who dared to appear on the dark streets, and their faces became dejected as they stared at the large printed posters.

"Why should we fight?" the men asked gloomily, for they saw no reason for a war. Nobody had done them any harm. They had always worked just so that others could make use of the things they produced. So the poor men grumbled and kept on asking, "Why must there be a war now? Nobody has harmed us!"

Some policemen, who were standing nearby, yelled at them and threatened them. "The king has ordered war, *basta!* You're not to question what he commands. Go home and get ready! March!"

The poor men lifted their heads and looked at the two policemen. They were fat, red, and arrogant.

"If we must go to war, our families will have nothing more to eat," the poor men said. Then the two fat officers drew their large clubs and yelled even louder: "Get out of here! There's going to be a war whether you like it or not!"

And since none of the poor men had a weapon, since everyone was tired, they trotted home, where the women had tears in their eyes. Many cursed the king. But the workers were tired. Their eyelids drooped and closed. Nobody wanted to fight. Sleep was what they wanted most.

Among the poor people was a man named Michael, who went from house to house telling all he met, "If that's the way they want it, then none of us will work tomorrow. We'll sneak secretly into the nearby woods. We'll stay away from the army barracks and wait to see what happens."

And all of the people agreed and followed his advice.

When the sun stood over the city the next day, there was nothing to be seen but rich people complaining and policemen running around the streets and looking for workers. There was no bread. The trains did not function. The cars were empty. The water did not run. The shops were closed. Money was of no use. Everything was closed and deadly quiet.

The rich people became terribly frightened. They jumped out of their sickbeds and ran out of the hospitals to storm the police station and city hall. They complained and demanded that people perform their work, that the bread be baked, that the cars and trains function, that there be water and wine and food and beer. But the mayor and the city councillors had sneaked out of the city. The policemen searched for them in vain. Then they closed ranks and marched into the workers' district shooting into the houses as they went by. But nobody seemed to be inside. Everything remained still.

Then the rich people became horrified. The policemen held their breath and asked helplessly, "Why? What's the meaning of all this?"

And nobody knew the answer. Finally they hit upon the bright idea of opening the prisons and forcing the prisoners to work. However, the prisoners refused to lift a hand. Even the worst sorts of threats did not help. The prisoners turned around and began to move out of the city. Then, when the policemen fired at them, they ran as fast as they could.

The rich people stood there, horrified again, with open mouths. The policemen stared dumbly, and finally they too ran helter-skelter out of the dismal city.

Two, three, and eventually four days passed. After a long ride the king came again and found everything abandoned. There was just an old crippled man who hobbled through a desolate alley toward him. He looked so gruesome that the king held his breath in horror and grabbed hold of his saber.

"Who are you?" the tyrant yelled at the ghastly man who stood still and rickety and gaped at him with glossy eyes.

"I'm the one who doesn't fear you!" the old man answered without a sign of praise.

"What!" the king bellowed and burned with anger. He drew his saber and wanted to hack at the old man. However, the figure of the old man suddenly sprang into the sky like a spiral spring, and he now bent his head, which hung on a long eerie neck, down toward the king. There was a smirk on his lips. "Go ahead and strike!" he said.

As though paralyzed by fright, the king let his arm sink, for now, once the gigantic face was near his, he recognized the man he had shot in the mouth many years ago. "Who are you?" he gasped feebly. "For God's sake, who are you?"

"I am the terror, misery, and injustice that you have spread!" The powerful head, which was hanging and swaying in the air, screamed into the face of the king. And suddenly, two gigantic bony arms extended themselves and gradually clutched the king, who begged fearfully for mercy. The large skull opened its mouth wide, and when the king looked down the dark throat, it was as if he saw all of the people whom he had senselessly slaughtered—the murdered subjects, the victims he had sentenced to death, the starved people, the miserable ones, and the insulted creatures, all who had suffered under his rule.

"Do you see these people? Do you see them all? You shall beg for mercy from each one of these thousands upon thousands of people, you mighty vain king! They are countless, and until you have finished with the count, you must starve and suffer like all of them!" Such was the cry of the voice that came out of the throat. Then the gigantic ghost disappeared with the king, and they landed deep underneath the earth in the most terrible hell. There the tyrant met all of those like him who had ruled as they had pleased, and they all groaned and stared at the red hot landscape and continually counted their murdered subjects whom they had driven to death.

Since then there has been peace in the land.

Heinrich Schulz

The Castle with the Three Windows

(1924)

nce upon a time there was a king who had never been outside his castle. His ministers had told him that it was not appropriate for a king to live anywhere except in his castle, and in this castle there were three large windows that faced different sides. The windowpanes were unusual because the ministers had ordered the glass to be tinted each with a different color, and so each window had an extraordinary power.

One window was made of rose-red glass that magnified everything one saw through it. If one looked through this window, one could see a glorious castle in the distance, where the relatives of the ministers lived. The king always saw this castle glowing in beautiful rose-red light, and the people who went in and out of this gorgeous castle looked equally rosy and cheerful. Moreover, they appeared to be powerful and valiant creatures because of the window's magic.

The ministers would always say to the king, "See, those are your friends! Your ancestors came from those people, and therefore, they are the cream of your land."

In the second window there were bright blue panes made out of ordinary glass so that everything appeared in its normal size. It was only due to the distance that the people and objects seemed to be smaller than they were in reality. This window faced a city inhabited by good and obedient citizens.

The ministers would always say to the king, "See, they are second in the land. The people in the city are not as beautiful and as tall as your relatives in the rose-red castle. That is why they don't deserve to have as many rights as we have. They are smaller and don't understand as much as we do. Furthermore, their blue color is not as majestic as our red."

In the third window there were gray glass panes that reduced the size of everything one saw. When one looked through this window, one could see a large factory with many chimneys in the distance, and all around the factory there were many small and dirty houses and streets. And the people who went out of the small, dirty houses and into the large factory were like miserable, tiny ants who belonged in the narrow holes of the earth.

The ministers would always say to the king, "You see, they are not really human beings. They are called workers because they must work the entire day so that we others can live in dignity the way we deserve to live. These people are small, dirty, and dumb. That's why they don't deserve to have any rights at all."

The king believed everything his ministers told him because he had never heard anything else, nor had he ever seen the people and the world in any other way except through the three windows.

One day, however, the king saw a fly on the wall of his royal room. The fly irritated him, and he ordered it to disappear from the wall. But the fly didn't obey the king's order. It continued to enjoy itself by running up and down the wall. The king tried to shoo it away with his hand. However, the fly danced merrily away, circled around the room a few times, and then landed directly on the bald head of the king.

Since the king was just getting ready to hold an audience in his royal room, he became very angry at the fly that walked about his head so disrespectfully. He tried to whack it with his hand. But the fly saw the hand coming and managed to avoid it in time, so the king hit his own head. This made him even angrier. He grabbed his scepter and ran after the fly, which landed here and there and all over the place.

Bang! The king tried to hit it with his scepter as it was sitting on the edge of a precious vase and cleaning its wings. The vase fell to the floor in a thousand pieces while the fly remained untouched. Next the fly landed on a bottle of ink that was on the king's desk. As the king tried to hit it with his scepter again, the fly escaped and the ink splurted all over the desk and the official papers the king was supposed to sign that morning. The fly hummed merrily and headed now for the soft fur of the fat, white poodle lying comfortably on the hearth of the fireplace and sleeping soundly. The dog was dreaming just then about a juicy bone that the royal cook had given him, and he was snoring happily when all of a sudden— wham! The king's scepter landed rudely on his back, and he jumped up with a loud howl and squeal and limped away from the fireplace.

Now the king was terribly angry. He looked around the room in fury, searching for the fly. Then he saw it parading joyfully up and down the gray window. Like a wild man, the king raced toward the window and swung his scepter with all his might against the window pane.

Clink! Clink! Clack! Clack!

The glass shattered loudly, and the splinters whizzed in the air so that there was a buzzing in the king's ears. In the meantime the fly flew through the broken glass into the open and hummed merrily, while the king could only watch him soar away.

But his eyes saw something else now as well!

Right then the king forgot about the fly, the ink, the poodle, and the vase. The scepter fell from his hand onto the floor. He stood in front of the broken glass as though a spell had come over him, and he kept staring straight ahead.

What did he see?

He saw the factory with many chimneys and the houses surrounding the factory. However, the buildings were much larger than usual, not dark and dirty and narrow. In fact, they glistened in the bright sunshine. The

Heinrich Schulz, *Von Menschlein, Tierlein und Dinglein: Märchen aus dem Alltag* (Berlin: Dietz, 1924). Illustrator: Hans Baluschek. Tale: "The Castle with the Three Windows."

people who went in and out of the buildings were big and strong and had a brave way about them, so the king became really frightened. He stepped to the side of the window and looked through a piece of the remaining gray glass. The factory appeared to be dirty and depressing again, as it had normally appeared. The king realized now that it was only because of the windowpane that he imagined those people whom the ministers called workers to be so small and ugly.

He became furious and grabbed his scepter from the floor. He swung it angrily against the blue glass of the second window, which shattered to pieces. When he saw that the citizens of the city appeared to be blue only because of the glass, he took his scepter again and smashed the red window in fury.

Now the king was overwhelmed by what he saw! The castle was much smaller than he had imagined. And the people who walked and rode around the castle had conceited, feeble faces and were much smaller than they had seemed. Moreover, they didn't seem rosy and lively but pale, worn-out, and gray. So the king became very sad and shed bitter tears. He sat down on his throne and buried his face in his hands so that the round tears streamed through his thick fingers. And he pitied himself so much that he finally fell asleep out of pure self-pity.

When the ministers arrived and saw what had happened, they ordered all of the glassmakers of the land to come and replace the missing gray, blue, and red windowpanes that had been broken. After several hours, when the king awoke, his room seemed to be just as it used to be. So he believed that he had only dreamed about the fly and the broken windowpanes. And when he asked his ministers, they assured him convincingly that everything had just been a bad dream.

Anna Mosegaard

The Giant Spider

(1928)

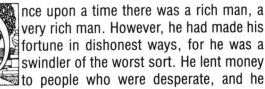 nce upon a time there was a rich man, a very rich man. However, he had made his fortune in dishonest ways, for he was a swindler of the worst sort. He lent money to people who were desperate, and he made them pay a great deal for the loans. Yet the more money he earned, the more restless he became. Soon it was impossible for him to relax and sleep at night. He constantly imagined himself in some sort of danger. Sometimes he believed that the banks in which he had deposited his money had gone bankrupt. Sometimes he imagined that a fire had broken out and had burned up his entire fortune. So he bought a fireproof safe for his money. Then he became afraid that thieves could break into his house, open the safe, and steal his money. So he collected all of his money and hid it in his bed. There were so many layers of money that he eventually needed a small ladder to climb up into his bed. The bumps in the mattress made it difficult for him to sleep, and his body became stiff. But that didn't matter, for now he was certain that nobody could steal his money during the night. As time passed, however, the bed became too uncomfortable for him. Therefore, he dragged his armchair to the side of the bed and sat there with a revolver in each of his hands. That was the way he stood watch over his dazzling fortune.

One night, when he began to doze, he dreamed that he was a young boy again and was sitting on his mother's lap. And his mother told him stories about giants, dwarfs, and the great mountain spirit, Rübezahl. Then suddenly, he was wakened by a loud explosion. He jumped up from his chair. Sweat poured down his forehead, and he looked around in fear. Had they come to rob him of his money? No, a revolver had slipped from his hand while he was asleep, and a shot had been fired. Right through the floor. It could easily have hit him! Plagued by thoughts of death, he paced back and forth in the room and thought about his wonderful dream. It had been so beautiful to see himself sitting on his mother's lap so innocently again. She had been telling him about the great Rübezahl, the mountain spirit. Strange! Why did those great spirits only live in the past? Why couldn't they be found today? It would be wonderful if Rübezahl were still alive and he could have the spirit guard his fortune. Then he could sleep in peace again.

The miser had to smile—and he didn't look bad with that smile! And the moon shone brightly through the window. What would it be like, he thought, if he set upon his way in this full moon, if he went into the woods to look for the mountain spirit. Yes, that was what he would do!

He took a large sack and stuffed it with his entire paper fortune and sneaked secretly from the house into the forest. As he walked alone through the woods, he became somewhat afraid. What if robbers were to come and take away his money! And the high cliffs, the dark evergreens, how eery they seemed in the silver moonlight!

When he finally reached the side of the mountain, he knocked loudly. Then, *knock! knock! knock!* came the echo in the forest. Nobody answered.

"Rübezahl, come out now if you want me to believe in you!" the miser scoffed at the mountain. His sarcastic laughter could still be heard when suddenly a mighty storm erupted in the woods, and a gigantic figure stood in front of him.

"Who are you?" the miser gasped and sank to his knees.

"It doesn't matter who I am!" the voice said, and it sounded as though it were the rumbling thunder itself.

"Are you Rübezahl?" The man was frightened to death.

"I am the mountain spirit—my name means nothing to you. But who are you, worm of the earth, and how dare you summon me?" the giant growled, and fire shot like lighting from his eyes.

"Me—me—my name's Greasman!" The miser trembled.

"Why have you come looking for me? Are you in trouble? Are you starving or dying from thirst?"

"No, that's not it exactly," the swindler said meekly.

Now he was in trouble, for he had forgotten something important that his mother had told him. The mountain spirit helped only poor, innocent people who had fallen into trouble—yes, that was it! The mountain spirit hated misers and swindlers like him.

"What do you want from me?" the mountain spirit roared with a booming voice.

"Look, O mighty spirit of the mountain," the swindler whimpered, "I have a bit of money, and I wanted to ask you to keep it safe for me—in the mountain underneath the earth. It will be safer there from thieves and fire!"

"Why don't you give some of your money to poor people if you have so much that you're afraid it will be stolen?"

The miser was too embarrassed to answer.

"Hm! Hm! Let me see the little bit of money you have!"

The mountain spirit stuck his hand inside the sack. He laughed as he whirled the money around, and a few million bank notes flew through the air.

"My money! My money!" the miser yelled and threw himself over the sack of money so that the bills could no longer escape from the large bag.

The mountain spirit laughed so hard that an echo resounded from the surrounding cliffs. "Well, give me the rest, and I'll protect your money for you. I'll be right back and bring you a receipt."

The miser heaved a sigh of relief.

It didn't take long for the mountain spirit to return, and he was carrying a large stuffed bag on his shoulder.

"Follow me!" the mountain spirit said. "I'll carry the sack to the edge of the woods. It's quite heavy. I've kept your paper bills and have filled the sack with gold and silver. Bury it at home in your cellar. It will be safe there from thieves and fire."

"Gold and silver?" The swindler's eyes glistened. "You're much too generous!"

They came to the edge of the woods. "There!" said the mountain spirit, and he loaded the sack on the back of the swindler.

"Have mercy on me!" the man exclaimed and sank to his knees. The sack was so heavy that he crumbled to the ground.

"Yes, it is somewhat heavy. I told you so, you crook! The tears of the poor people whom you cheated are hanging on each one of the coins, and their tears are what's making your burden so heavy."

"I can't bear this!" the miser gasped, and he wanted to throw the sack off his back, but it had become glued to him.

Laughter resounded through the forest. It was as if all of the trees and animals of the forest joined in the laughter. Suddenly the miser was alone. Like a beast he crawled on his hands and legs. The sack was glued to his back. Slowly, like a snail, he crawled forward. When he saw the city before him, he felt too ashamed to crawl there like a beast. After all he was a human being! So he crawled back into the forest.

Soon he began suffering from hunger, and all of his gold and silver could not help him now. He couldn't even stand up straight to pick apples or berries off a tree. When the hunger finally got the better of him, he grabbed some snails that had just crossed his path, and he stuck them in his mouth, although he felt repulsed by them. His thirst was now worse than his hunger. He seemed to hear a bubbling brook somewhere, and he crawled for hours along a path in the scorching sun, but he did not find the brook, just a deep waterhole. When he crawled to the edge and sought to wet his burning lips, he had to stop because the burden on his back shifted forward and threatened to push him over the edge into the water. That would have meant his death, so he crawled back into the forest. In order to reduce his thirst he licked the dewdrops from the grass that grew along the way.

One day, when he could no longer stand his hunger and thirst anymore, he crawled to the nearest village. There he stopped in front of a blacksmith. A group of young farmer boys came along and laughed and shouted when they saw him. "Look—look! A giant spider! It's a poison one for sure!" They prepared to beat him with their shovels and hoes. The swindler didn't dare budge. A giant spider. Yes, that is the way he probably looked with his long thin arms and legs and the stuffed sack of coins on his back.

Beat me, he thought; then my torture will end. But just at that moment the blacksmith rushed from the house and ordered the young men to stop. "Don't you see that it's a human being?" he said.

"No, it's a poison spider!" they answered.

"A poison spider can't cry! Don't you see the tears in his eyes?"

It was true! The poison spider was crying and asking for a drink of water. The blacksmith brought him food and something to drink.

"Thank you," the swindler said with emotion. "Open my sack and take as much silver and gold as you want for your reward."

"I don't want a reward!" the blacksmith replied.

"But I'm grateful for every coin a person takes. This burden weighs me down!" the swindler said.

So the blacksmith obliged him. However, the swindler was astonished when the blacksmith held a handful of old iron pieces under his nose and laughed. "So this is your gold and silver! If you want to sell it, I'll gladly give you two pennies for a pound."

The miser saw now that the mountain spirit had tricked him. He was so shaken by this that he suddenly keeled over and died. And since the people could not believe that he was a real human being, they refused to bury him in the cemetery. Instead, they dug a grave for him on the side of the road.

Animal Wisdom

Robert Grötzsch

Felix the Fish

elix the fish was a—wait, this beginning is wrong. I'll try again. In olden days it so happened—no, that's not the way either. This story begins like all really good fairy tales. Once upon a time there was a giant whose name was Adolf. It so happened that he came from the distant mountains down into the valley one time to wash his legs in the Elbe River, and he liked the river so much that he settled down on its banks for good, right on the river's banks where most of the people lived. That was where he made his home, and soon one farmer found a cow missing; another, a horse; and another, all of his fodder. The giant had an enormous appetite, and he grabbed everything he could lay his hands on.

All that would not have been so terrible if the giant Adolf had not also had an annoying habit that was worse than anything else. On hot days he laid himself right across the River Elbe so that his powerful body blocked the flow of the water. The waves could not spring over his body, and the river overflowed the banks and spread throughout the neighboring countryside. The fields and gardens became swamps, and the ships could not continue their journeys on the river. The farmers, craftsmen, and seafarers all complained: "The giant's destroying everything! If he would only drown!"

But he didn't drown, for whoever stays alert never drowns. And the people could not kill him because they were much too afraid and did not dare go near the monstrous fellow. They only complained, day after day.

A fish heard all of this. His name was Felix, not Sunny Boy or Bright Eyes but Felix. He felt sorry for the people,

Robert Grötzsch, *Der Zauberer Burufu* (Berlin: Dietz, 1922). Illustrator unknown. Tale: "Felix the Fish."

who were in a terrible plight, and he swore: "I'll get rid of the giant for them."

And really, one day when the giant laid himself across the river, Felix the fish swam way out and then took off toward the giant with all of his might. He soared and hit him under the arm where he was ticklish, right there where Adolf was most ticklish.

"Damn it!" screeched the giant, and he splashed wildly with his arms and legs and grabbed Felix in a hand that was as large as a house. But—swish!—the little fish slipped through the powerful fingers and jumped into the water, and away he went!

However, the giant had seen the devilish fish. "Just you wait!" Adolf laughed fiercely. "Just you wait. I'll get you yet!"

Felix answered with a cheerful spring into the air. Then he sped home to his mother. "You see, what did I tell you?" his mother warned him. "Don't start up with the giant!" But Felix shot over to the bank where the people were sitting and cursing the harmful giant.

As he swam toward the people, Felix began yelling, "Feed me so I can become big and strong. Then I'll get rid of the giant for you!"

Many other fish heard this, and they swam toward the shore, and each one yelled, "Feed me so I can become big and strong. Then I'll get rid of the giant for you!"

The people looked at them and said, "That's a good idea! A strong fish can do many things we can't!" And they began examining the fish who had gathered there.

One fish, by the name of Floating Freddy, was most impressive. He was a large powerful carp whose stout body completely overshadowed little Felix. "The stout carp is perfect," the people said. "Bring Master Wit to us!"

Master Wit was considered to be very smart because he could do incredible things with all kinds of pills. When he arrived and eyed the carp, he said, "He doesn't seem to be the right one to me. But do as you like!"

Whereupon he signaled the stout fish to come to the shore, and he gave him a pill to swallow that had the color of a violet sunset. Then he placed his hand on the fish's head and said, "Knackle, dackle, wackle! Razzle, dazzle, prazzle!"

From then on the stout Floating Freddy led a wonderful life. He would lie near the bank where the people fed him the finest tidbits, which he swallowed in enormous quantities, and thus he grew to be as tremendous as a whale. But he did not grow just long and strong. He became especially fat, round, and bulky. His eyes were gradually swollen in blubber. His belly touched the bottom of the river, and his movements became more and more sluggish as he became lazy and slack. After several weeks the people came to him and urged him to fight. "Now that we've built you up with enormous amounts of food," they said, "it's time for you to destroy the giant!"

Floating Freddy wagged his tail lazily, wobbled his gills wearily, and pouted. "Wait until the moon changes. I still feel very weak." And his enormous belly demanded more food every day.

However, there came a time when Floating Freddy waited in vain for his food. Instead, the people were boiling mad and yelled at him: "Now's the time to destroy the monster, you lazy floating beast! The giant's been lying in the river for a week, and the land is flooded. Our ships can't move any further. Our fields are swamped. Our houses are being carried away. Destroy this monster once and for all; otherwise we won't give you one more handful of food!" They promised him his tidbits only after he returned victorious from a fight with the giant.

Finally, the stout, gigantic fish made all sorts of preparations to begin the fight. But because he had lain there so lazily for such a long time, it was difficult for him to swim. Nevertheless, after splashing about, he managed to reach the middle of the river. Then he did all sorts of little things to make himself seem important. He sneezed, spat, and swallowed awkwardly. He asked with a yawn whether the riverbed was free for him to roll for his takeoff. He puffed up his gills and prepared for the takeoff, then suddenly steamed back to the shore, gasped for breath, and moaned, "Wait one more day . . . I feel too weak today. Feed me."

But this time Floating Freddy had miscalculated. The people on the banks did not say a word. They grabbed stones and threw them at the sluggish fish. When Floating Freddy realized how bad things were for him, and when he felt the stones hit him as thick as hail, he began to scream: "Stop! Stop! I'll start the fight right away. I just wanted to gather my strength for a moment." Then Floating Freddy really and truly steered himself to the middle of the river, panted, swallowed, spat, coughed, and snorted. When his fins flipped and flapped, he gradually began to move. He swam faster and faster until, propelled by his blubber, he soared toward the giant.

Adolf was lying straight and flat across the River Elbe and was consuming a cow when he saw the massive gigantic fish coming. He reacted by merely lifting his enormous head a bit, laughing, and shaking his powerful fist in a threatening way. This was enough to cause Floating Freddy to slow down visibly. He applied the brakes to his fins, and his movements became slower and slower and then—Then the horrified people on shore saw that Floating Freddy—that powerful gilled fish—that coward slowly and carefully made a circle around the giant's head and helped himself generously to the remains of the cow.

From then on there was not only one monster blocking the Elbe but two who loafed about in the river— Adolf and Floating Freddy. They lay side by side spread across the river, lodged between the banks, and spent their time talking, feasting, and causing mischief.

The people moaned and complained: "First we fed the fish until he became fat, and now we have two gigantic loafers in the river!"

Robert Grötzsch, *Der Zauberer Burufu* (Berlin: Dietz, 1922). Illustrator unknown. Tale: "Felix the Fish."

152

Felix the fish heard this. He swam to the shore and scolded the people. "Why didn't you feed me so I could become big. I would have driven the giant away!" And Felix's mother flapped her gills, cried out, and raised a storm: "I told you so!" But Felix raised his head from the water and demanded, "Make me big and strong; then I'll chase them both away."

However, the people laughed bitterly, "You little fish. You twirp! We have even less to gain with you than with Floating Freddy!"

It was really fortunate that Master Wit happened to be nearby. He raised his finger in warning. "Friends, we must try again! This fish seems to be the one. He's got the right look in his eyes!"

"All right, let's try again," the people said. "We'll try again if Master Wit believes that this fish has the right look in his eyes!"

The Master really believed that, and he waved Felix to approach the bank. Then he gave him a pill to swallow that was the color of the red sunrise, and he placed his hand on the fish's head. "Knackle, dackle, wackle! Razzle, dazzle, prazzle!"

From then on a totally new life began for Felix. He ate for ten people and grew bigger each day, more robust, stronger, and powerful. He could hardly wait for the fight with the giant, and he ate entirely out of enthusiasm. The people, who watched the feedings from the shore, looked into the clear water and saw how Felix spread himself a bit longer with each bite. What was especially pleasing for the people to see was the fact that the brave fish did not become as fat as Floating Freddy. On the contrary, Felix became firm and solid, not too fat and not too thin—just right, as a real fish should be. For Felix did not lie about on his scales day after day. Rather, he practiced enormous swim exercises every day and moved around so enthusiastically that he sometimes could not even bring himself to rest. Whenever the people groaned about the two who blocked the river,

Felix would then insist that the fight begin immediately. He had to be calmed down by Master Wit, who warned him: "Grow! Grow! Patience is strength! Adolf and Floating Freddy are not about to run away. Wait, think, click!"

But one day, when Adolf and Floating Freddy had stolen some cows from the farmers and had eaten them, Felix could no longer be held back. "Clear the ships from the river! Clear the river! I can't hold back anymore!" he yelled to the people. He whipped the water with his splendid body and steamed up the river a bit for his mighty takeoff. Then he turned around and shot downstream with furious speed. He had become such a truly imposing fish that the people followed his daring act with bated breath.

Adolf and Floating Freddy were lying straight across the river as Felix shot toward them with his head slightly lifted in a threatening way. Floating Freddy wanted to speed away while Adolf tried to get ready for the fight. Both failed. Their gigantic bodies had become so blubbery from all of their tremendous loafing that they could only turn on their sides—just as the wild Felix crashed into them!

His onslaught was terrifyingly beautiful!

The crowd of breathless people watched Felix cut Adolf and Floating Freddy into four separate pieces, and the four gigantic ruins drifted lifelessly downstream. But the daring victor was nowhere to be seen.

His takeoff had been so powerful that Felix could not slow down the force of his body. His motion sent him flying along the river into the open sea and straight across the ocean to America, where the gigantic fish bounced off the coast with a tremendous impact. That caused an earthquake, and his face became so swollen that an American doctor had to bandage it. Felix thanked the doctor and zoomed home again across the ocean and then southward down the Elbe. When his mother, who had swum a bit upstream, caught sight of her bandaged son, her eyes widened and she declared, "You see, I told you so!"

But Felix splashed cheerfully with his fins, for the river was now freed of the monsters. The people stood happily on the banks of the river, and they all applauded him so enthusiastically that he never forgot that beautiful day as long as he lived.

Edwin Hoernle

The Poodle and the Schnauzer
(1920)

he dogs were tired of obeying the humans. They wanted to be free like the wolves in the woods. So one bright, moonlit night they held a meeting to decide what steps they should take. "Let's declare war against the humans!" they shouted unanimously, but they were divided about the way to conduct their war.

After arguing back and forth for some time the learned poodle began to speak. "Dogs," he exclaimed, "Observe the humans! How is it that they've become powerful? Isn't it due to their wise devices and instruments? They used them to trick and tame our fathers, and they use them now to keep us in chains and to terrify and suppress us constantly—they who are weaker by nature. What are we to make of this, dogs? I say that we must learn to conduct ourselves like them, to use instruments and devices like theirs. We must prove to them that we are their equals. Then they will respect and fear us and will not deny us our equal rights."

The dogs all agreed with the poodle's depiction of the situation. "He's right, yes, he's definitely right!" the entire chorus howled. "Let the poodle be our leader!"

Such respect shown to the poodle annoyed the schnauzer. "I'm only a simple stable dog," he snarled. "I prefer to take the short, straight path."

"Well then, tell us what you think," the dogs cried out.

The schnauzer pounded his breast and bared his teeth. "I'm only a simple stable dog," he began, "and I don't have the poodle's skills. On the other hand, I have a sharp bite, and I have the highly developed, fine instinct of a dog. This is something I can depend upon. Or do you think, my worthy fellow dogs, that the humans will not notice the poodle's intentions and will not be able to prevent him in time from realizing them?"

The schnauzer looked about him in triumph.

"He's got a point there," barked a large hound who had plenty of experience.

"I'm sure the humans will stop him," the schnauzer continued. "Or do you believe that they lock us in miserable dog huts for nothing while they themselves live in warm, comfortable houses. No, dogs, the humans will never allow us to become as wise and powerful as they are."

The schnauzer paused momentarily to observe the effect of his words. Then he raised his voice again. "Let us have faith only in our strong bite," he exclaimed, "and in our grim jaws! Let us show the humans our teeth!"

The schnauzer's militant speech made an impression. "He's right, yes, he's definitely right," the chorus of dogs shouted. "Let the schnauzer be our leader!"

Then they all returned home, each one to his leash.

Time passed. The dogs gathered in the woods again on a bright, moonlit night. "What did you accomplish?" they asked the poodle.

The poodle sprang proudly into the middle of the circle. He begged, stood on his hind legs, and sprang through a hoop. "See what a sharp poodle I am!" he cried. "I learned all that from the humans."

"And what have you gained from all this?" the dogs asked.

"The human has taken me into his house," the poodle answered. "Now I eat under his table and sleep at the foot of his bed. Sometimes he scratches me behind the ears and pets my fur. Soon I'll get even more than that."

The dogs gazed upon the poodle with admiration. "His words are good," the large hound with experience said. "In fact, his words are very good. But let us hear the schnauzer as well."

The schnauzer entered the ring. "What's the use of developing the poodle's skills," he began, "as long as we are threatened with the whip every day? Let the poodle dare take a piece of meat by himself from the master's dish when he's hungry. What do you think the human will do then?"

"He'll use the whip and throw the poodle out the door," the dogs cried.

"Yes, that's what he'll do," the schnauzer said, "and more than that. He'll beat him until he bleeds in spite of all his begging, standing on his hind feet, springing through hoops, and offering his paw. As far as I'm concerned, I'd be ashamed to say that I've won the favor of a human."

"But what should we do?" the dogs bellowed.

"Do?" the schnauzer asked with emphasis. "We'll defend ourselves. We'll bark when the human comes too close to us. If he attempts to put us on a leash, we'll bite his hand. If he beats us, we'll grab hold of his pants!" That made sense to the dogs.

"His words are good," the schnauzer's friends exclaimed. "In fact, they are very good."

No sooner did they say this than a violent argument arose among the dogs. Some supported the poodle and his tricks, and some stood behind the schnauzer and his biting.

When it became apparent they would not come to an agreement, they all ran home, each to his leash.

Time rushed by, and the situation of the dogs did not become an iota better than before. On the contrary. The human made a stick out of hazel wood, and he used it to beat the poodle when the dog refused to perform his tricks. The poodle had to beg, walk on his hind legs, and jump through hoops the entire day. The human gave the poodle to his children as a present, and they laughed until they burst. The schnauzer, too, met with misfortune. His bark made no impression on the humans. When he snapped at the human's hand, the human bought a muzzle. "Now, you'll learn to behave yourself, buddy," the human sneered. Then he punished the schnauzer by locking him in the yard when the weather turned cold and rainy.

Dejected and defeated, the dogs gathered for a third time in the woods on a bright, moonlit night. The poodle gave his most glorious speech, but nobody listened anymore. The schnauzer spoke about barking and biting, but he wore a muzzle and cut a ridiculous figure. The situation was critical. The opinions whizzed confusedly through the air. Some urged that the dogs should strike and stop giving birth to puppies. If there were fewer and fewer dogs on earth, perhaps the humans would stop torturing them. Others demanded that they steal the humans' Bible because it had given them the idea that they were the crown of all creation.

Finally, the dogs separated, each to his leash.

A wolf who had listened attentively to the speeches of the dogs shook his head. "Strange," he said, "that dogs waste so much time and words on incidental matters. They only have to stay here in the woods to be free."

"You speak like a wolf," a wild pigeon scoffed at him from a high tree. "You've managed to grow large and big through fights and danger. You like to hunt your food by yourself. You're willing to starve for your freedom, even to die for it. But dogs love an orderly life and the bones that are tossed to them."

"That's exactly why they are dogs," growled the wolf and went his way.

Edwin Hoernle

The Chameleon

(1920)

nce there was a panther who hid in a thicket to catch his breath because some hunters were hard on his heels. Suddenly, he heard a voice from the branches above his head.

"Hee, hee, hee," the voice chuckled. "Didn't I tell you? Even with your terrible claws and your gigantic roar you'll come to a horrible end. You were never smart enough to learn how to adapt to the given conditions. Look how meek the strong panther is now!"

The panther looked round him, but he couldn't find the owner of the gloating voice. There were only green leaves and branches waving in the wind. He was about to move on his way when the voice spoke again.

"I feel sorry for you, dear panther, but nobody can help you now. When there was still time, you wouldn't listen. Look at me! While you boasted with all your strength and made an enemy of the entire world, I made an effort to learn from the conditions. So now I can easily assume any color or shade. That's why people leave me alone and they hunt you. I grow and prosper while you and your kind are being exterminated. Knowing how to adapt yourself, my dear panther, that's the way to gain some welfare in this world."

The panther shook himself. He was disgusted by this foolish talk, "Who are you?" he shouted unwillingly into the bushes.

"I'm the chameleon," the voice giggled, "from the family of reptiles. I've learned to change my color whenever I'm in danger. I always adapt to my environment.

That's the way I protect myself and trick the hunters, and that's how I poach upon insects."

Now the panther was finally able to perceive the ugly beast. It had assumed the color of the green leaves and was crawling slowly on top of a branch. It was waiting to ambush small insects, which it snatched by stealthily sticking out its wormlike tongue.

The panther raised himself. He licked his wounds and his beautiful fur, stretched his powerful body, and showed his claws.

"What are you going to do?" The chameleon became frightened on its perch.

"I see the hunters coming, and I'm going to meet them," the panther responded calmly.

"Are you crazy?" the chameleon cried. "That's pure suicide. They'll shoot you down. Follow my example and hide under the branches! Look how cleverly I can match the color of this wood. As soon as the danger passes, I'm the same old me again."

"That's why you're a chameleon," the panther answered, "but that's why I'm proud to come from the family of the tigers." Upon saying this he was off with a mighty leap.

Before the hunters who were creeping closer could realize what had happened, the panther clawed some of them to the ground and broke through their ring. Later, when he granted himself some rest again, he was surrounded by the glorious freedom of boundless hills and woods.

But what happened to the chameleon?

A German professor who happened to be with the hunters is supposed to have caught it and taken it home with him. People say that he gave this harmless animal to his little nephew as a gift to wile away the time.

The little boy delighted himself in observing the artistic skill of the clever animal. If it sat on a piece of red cloth, then he would force it to move to a violet one, then blue, and finally black. The chameleon changed its color promptly with each new background.

The German professor and his little nephew praised the perfectionism and cleverness of the good animal.

However, one day its doom drew near.

The professor went out, and the little nephew was left alone in the house. The boy placed a plaid scarf on the table and wanted the chameleon to demonstrate his skills.

The nice, obedient animal, accustomed only to adapting itself to each new situation, tried its best now too. However, it was impossible to assume all of the colors at the same time.

It's said that the chameleon died from overexertion.

Felix Fechenbach

The Triumph of the Wolves

(c. 1925)

hen the war between the wild animals and wild birds came to an end and the domestic animals, who had fought on the side of the wild animals, were once again persecuted by the wild ones as in previous times, they eventually lost their patience. So one day the domestic animals rebelled with great animosity, and they told the lion, along with all of his councillors—who represented all of the different kinds of wild animals—to go to the devil. A great council of domestic animals was elected to take care of the government in the animal kingdom. The lion, who had ruled as king until then, was banished to a distant cave.

However, since domestic animals tend to be sentimental, they decided that the horses, former subjects of the lion, had to bring him something to eat each day. They felt that it was not right to let a banished king starve.

Then they attempted to restore everything to its right place.

In the animal kingdom it was an old custom to celebrate a day of justice once a year. The wolves functioned as judges and the jackals as prosecutors. The young among the domestic animals demanded that the important posts of judge and prosecutor be placed in the hands of the domestic animals. But the old sheep, oxen, and donkeys argued for maintaining the traditional forms, and they especially did not want to abandon the constitutional principle regarding the immutability of the wolves. Moreover, they claimed that it was impossible to fill these posts with domestic animals because the sheep, oxen, and donkeys could never be anything but domestic animals even if they were appointed judges.

The old animals pushed through their position, and the wolves remained judges, and the jackals, prosecutors.

As the day of justice approached, the wolves planned a secret conspiracy with the jackals and other wild animals against the domestic animals, who arrived unsuspectingly in large hordes and proud of their newly won power.

However, as the last donkey came to the place of justice, the jackals accused all of the domestic animals of high treason, and the wolves came to a quick decision: the accused were to serve as food for the wild animals.

Before the domestic animals could really grasp what was actually happening, they were torn to pieces by the wild animals and eaten. Then the banished lion returned in triumph to his throne in the animal kingdom.

Of course, the wolves were given high titles and decorated with medals.

Felix Fechenbach

The Revolution in the Zoo
(c. 1925)

n a large city there was a splendid zoological garden with numerous animals, all in
iron cages and tended by guards. A director supervised everything.

The animals felt their condition of enslavement and imprisonment to be humiliating and de-
grading. For a long time the inhabitants of the zoo had
been seething, and one day they could no longer repress
their bitter feelings. They exploded. The lions and tigers,
the leopards and wolves, the bears and monkeys, and
even the camels and donkeys—in short, any and everything that had legs—broke out of their cages.

The guards were greatly alarmed and rushed with
whips, poles, and spears to drive the animals back into
their prisons. But they could not control the beasts, and
eventually the furious animals drove them away, along
with their director.

Now the animals gathered together and elected a sov-
ereign parliament according to the rules of proportional
representation, and the parliament was to determine
what was to be done. All kinds of animals were represented in this parliament. Even the donkeys and the
camels, who made themselves especially prominent
during the deliberations. In order to make a fine appearance, they put on horn-rimmed glasses and looked like
professors from a learned college.

The result of the parliament's deliberations was a
unanimously accepted resolution, which declared that
the park in which the animals lived was not a zoological
garden but a free state of the animals in which the ani-

mals could determine their own destiny by the strength of their laws.

A donkey who was versed in writing drafted the resolution on paper in an elegant, neat fashion. Then he made a large plaque with the wording of the resolution printed on it in forceful antique letters. A camel, who had an especially long neck, hung the plaque over the entrance of the zoo.

The parliament elected by the animals met continually and held endless deliberations and debates aimed at creating a constitution for the free state of the animals. However, the deliberations lasted so long that the guards, who had been driven away, had time to reassemble. And because the animals had neglected to take away their whips, poles, and spears, the guards could suddenly attack the unsuspecting animals during their deliberations, and they drove the beasts back into their cages.

Then the director, who had also returned, assumed control of the zoo again.

The animals now lived as before in a condition of enslavement unworthy of animals. Everything was just as it had ever been when the guards ruled. The only thing that was different was the plaque that hung over the entrance of the zoo, and one could read the following printed in large antique letters:

THIS PARK IS NOT A ZOOLOGICAL GARDEN BUT A FREE STATE OF ANIMALS IN WHICH THE ANIMALS DETERMINE THEIR OWN DESTINY BY STRENGTH OF THEIR OWN LAWS!

Felix Fechenbach

The Chameleon
(c. 1925)

statesman kept a chameleon in his country villa to trap and devour the countless flies.

One day a large group of gentlemen were invited to the villa as guests, and they had lively discussions about political events and politicians. One of the conversations concerned a politician adept at switching his positions, and consequently he was generally referred to as the political chameleon.

Meanwhile the four-footed chameleon sat in a corner and listened to the stories about this man dubbed with his name. This seemed very strange to him. So he waited patiently until the last guest had left the villa, and then he asked his master about the two-footed relative.

"You have the ability," the statesman answered, "to change the color of your skin to fit your mood or situation. Sometimes you're green, yellow, pink, or sky blue. However, the man about whom you are inquiring knows how to represent the political views of one or the other group as if they were his own, so he has already radiated almost as many colors as there are parties. It's because of this kind of multiple coloring that we've named him a political chameleon."

This answer made the sensitive animal extremely irritated, and he wanted to dispute this comparison. "My play with colors is purely artificial. I put on a different color of coat but only to a certain extent, and in the process I do not change my character or my principles. But your politician with many colors must constantly change his character and principles whenever he switches colors."

"You're wrong," the statesman said. "The political chameleon changes neither character nor principles when he switches colors."

"Why is that?" the naive animal wanted to know.

"Because he has never had one or the other in the first place," the experienced statesman calmly answered.

Béla Illés

The Fairy Tale about the Bear, the Wolf and the Sly Fox

(1925)

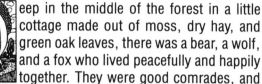eep in the middle of the forest in a little cottage made out of moss, dry hay, and green oak leaves, there was a bear, a wolf, and a fox who lived peacefully and happily together. They were good comrades, and they got up in the evening and went to bed in the morning. They ate meat, drank milk, nibbled honey, played, and sang together. And even when they chanced to quarrel with the moon every now and then because they were in a bad mood, their quarrel never ended catastrophically, for the moon never answered them rudely. In general, the three friends led a pleasant life.

Once during the course of a beautiful morning the three comrades wandered much too far from their dwelling, and they caught sight of a man wearing a top hat at the edge of the forest.

"A hunter," the wolf said. "Grrr, how I hate these men!"

"It's not a hunter," the bear remarked. "He's not carrying a rifle." And he formed a telescope with his paws so that he could see better.

"Ha, ha, ha!" the fox laughed. "That's not a man standing there. It's just the clothes of a man pulled over some long sticks to look like a man. If I'm correctly informed, this plaything is called a scarecrow."

"It seems that you're right," said the wolf, who had wolf's eyes, and now he could see clearly that the clothes, which were draped over sticks, were tied together and were dangling in the wind.

"If you're so smart, brother," the wolf said, turning to the fox, then you might tell us what the purpose of this plaything is."

"I think the good men set up scarecrows in the fields so that the birds can see from a distance where they can find something good to eat."

"That's nice of them!" said the bear. He was the first to arrive at the scarecrow, which was patched together with two long sticks, a jacket, pants, and a beaten-up top hat that was slightly dented. The fox took the top hat and put it on his own head.

"Don't I look handsome?" he asked laughingly.

The wolf and the bear nodded, and since they were merry fellows, the wolf slipped into the jacket and the bear into the pants.

"Friends"—the fox was the first to speak again— "now that we have slipped into the skin of human beings, let us venture further and see what it's like to mix with humans a little. There are three paths that lead from the spot on which we are standing. Let's separate now for a short time, and in three days from now we'll meet at home and compare notes."

The other two found the proposal a good idea, and they immediately set out on their way: the wolf to the left, the bear straight ahead, the fox to the right.

The wolf hummed a merry marching song and made his way through the woods. The thorny bushes tried to bar his way. The birds laughed at him. However, he was firm as a rock and pursued his path undisturbed by all of this. After he had trudged through the woods for some three hours, a man dressed in a green uniform with silver buttons and a silver spiked helmet yelled, "Stop!"

This man was wearing a saber on his side, and he held a rubber club in his hand. "Where are you heading, country boy?"

"To the city," the wolf replied.

"Are you poor?"

"Y-y-yes," the wolf stuttered, for he wasn't sure what the green man meant by this question.

"Are you looking for work?" inquired the green man, who began to play with his saber while he spoke.

"Y-y-yes," replied the wolf, who became somewhat uneasy as the green man continued to play with his saber.

"You've come to the right place then," the green man said and motioned to the wolf to follow him. The green man led him into a large yellow building where the noise was so loud that the wolf slumped his shoulders and covered his ears. Then he was directed into a room where a gigantic red and white machine rattled and puffed out such suffocating gas between grinding wheels that the wolf didn't dare open his mouth. That was how unbelievably frightened he was. Then his hind legs were bound by strong straps to a huge wheel of the machine.

"Pull!" the green man shouted at the wolf, and he delivered some hard blows to the wolf's back with the rubber club.

The wolf used all of his muscles and pulled and pulled with all his might. Yet no matter how much he exerted himself, the green man kept on yelling in his ears, and each yell was accompanied by a blow of the rubber club. Hours went by, and the machine produced cartloads of shoes, clothes, hats, scythes, pitchforks, and spades. Friend Wolf was so dizzy from hunger that he no longer knew whether he was male or female. When the straps were finally taken off him, the wolf collapsed from exhaustion.

"You're hungry, aren't you, country boy?" the green man asked.

"I'm as hungry as a wolf," replied the wolf.

"Then eat, country boy," the green man said, and he gave the wolf six pumpkin seeds.

"You're probably tired as well, country boy?" the green man asked again.

"I'm as tired as a dog," replied the wolf.

"Then take a break, but no longer than ten minutes."

For two days and two nights Friend Wolf was treated as miserably as a dog. On the third day, however, he stuck out his tongue, lay down, and didn't care whether or not he was beaten. Indeed, the green man beat him furiously, but the wolf refused to budge, and the man became exhausted. So he called a small bald-headed man with glasses for advice. The bald-headed man felt the wolf's fur and examined his tail and ears. When he was finished, he coughed and delivered his opinion.

"The poor thing has lost all his strength. We can't let him work here anymore or he'll die on the spot, and we'll have to pay for his burial."

Upon hearing this, the green man untied the wolf from the straps, made a long slash in the wolf's fur with his saber, and then took the fur clean off the wolf's body with his quick hands. The wolf was so horrified that he couldn't protect himself.

"Come, my poor man," the green man said to the wolf, and he dragged him by the ears to the door, gave him a kick in the behind, and sent him on his way.

The wolf's entire body ached from the work, the blows, and the hunger. Most of all, however, he suffered because his fur was missing. What would his comrades think of him when he returned home nude?

But his comrades had suffered the same kind of fate. At least, the bear did. The bear had strolled away sprightfully and hummed a merry marching song. The thorny bushes tried to bar his way. The birds laughed at him. However, he was firm as a rock and pursued his path undisturbed by all of this. After he had trudged through the woods for some three hours, a man dressed in a blue uniform and a golden storm helmet yelled, "Stop!"

This man was wearing a thick saber at his side, and

he held a rifle with a bayonet in his hand. "Where are you heading, country boy?"

"Hm," answered the bear, who was somewhat unsettled by the saber and the rifle.

"Are you poor?"

"Hm," answered the bear.

"Are you looking for work?" the blue man continued to inquire.

"Y-y-yes!" the bear responded.

"Then you've come to the right spot," said the blue man, and he motioned the bear to follow him. They stopped at a very large field densely covered with beautiful ears of golden corn. The blue men tied a huge, thick chain to a tree at the edge of the field, and he tied the other end of the chain to the bear's hind legs. Then he drew his saber from the sheath and whacked the bear with the flat side on his back.

"Pull!" the blue man yelled and kept hitting the bear.

"Grrr!" the bear roared and began to pull. The blows of the saber were extremely painful, but since the bear was as strong as a bear, he flexed his muscles and pulled so hard that all of the ears of golden corn were dragged to the barn within a few hours. Then the blue man took the chain from the bear's hind legs and placed the tip of his bayonet on the bear's chest.

"You're hungry, aren't you, country boy?" the blue man asked.

"I'm as hungry as a bear," replied the bear.

"Then eat, country boy," the blue man said, and he gave the bear three sunflower seeds.

"You're probably tired as well, country boy?" the blue man asked again.

"I'm as tired as a dog," replied the bear.

"Then take a break, but no longer than two minutes."

After two short minutes the blue man led the bear to an immense forest. The forest was filled with tall trees that towered into the sky. The blue man tied a huge thick chain to a tree at the edge of the forest. Then he tied the other end of the chain to the hind legs of the bear. He drew his saber from its sheath and began to whack the bear again with the flat side on his back.

For two days and two nights Friend Bear was treated as miserably as a dog. On the third day, however, he stuck out his tongue, lay down, and didn't care whether he was shoved and beaten. He simply wouldn't work. Indeed, the blue man beat him furiously, but the bear refused to budge, and the man became exhausted. So he called a small bald-headed man with glasses for advice. The bald-headed man felt the bear's fur and examined his tail and ears. When he was finished, he coughed and delivered his opinion.

"The poor thing has lost all his strength. We can't let him work here anymore or he'll die on the spot, and we'll have to pay for his burial."

Upon hearing this, the blue man took the chain off the bear's hind legs, made a long slash in the bear's fur with his saber, and then took the fur clean off the bear's body with his quick hands. The bear was so horrified that he couldn't protect himself.

"Come, my poor man," the blue man said to the bear, and he dragged him by the ears until they reached the country road. There he gave him a kick in the behind and sent him on his way.

The bear's entire body ached from the work, the blows, and the hunger. Most of all, however, he suffered because his fur was missing. What would his comrades think of him when he returned home nude?

Indeed, he didn't have to rack his brains very long about that because he met his friend the wolf at the next crossing, and the wolf had just as little with which to cover his body as the bear had. Neither of them uttered a word. They were in a hurry to get home. But after arriving home and spending the entire day waiting in vain for the fox, the tender-hearted bear suddenly burst into tears.

"Our poor friend fox!" the bear sobbed, and he couldn't stop the tears. "I'm sure that they've not only taken his fur but also his life."

"We really should have looked after the poor fellow. He was so young and good."

This poor fellow, so young and good—that is, the fox—had begun the same way as the wolf and the bear. He had hummed a merry marching song and made his way through the woods. Thorny bushes had tried to bar his way. The birds had laughed at him. However, he was as firm as a rock, made a nose at them, and pursued his path. After he had trudged through the woods for some three hours, a man dressed in a velvet uniform and a checkered cap yelled, "Stop!"

This man was carrying a revolver, and he had a little whistle in his mouth. "Where are you heading, country boy?"

"That depends," replied the fox, who was a keen observer of human nature. He pointed to his top hat, which he had carefully polished along the way so that it was now bright and shining.

"Are you poor?"

"Not at all," replied the fox.

"Do you desire work?"

"Do you think I'm crazy?" the fox answered as if he were insulted. "Tell me, my dear man," the fox continued, and he placed his hand on the velvet man's shoulder. "Tell me quickly where the next garage is. My car crashed on this bumpy road and was smashed to pieces."

"At your service, my lord!" the velvet man answered, and he blew his whistle. A limousine appeared, and the fox stepped into it. He leaned back on the fine leather seat and with a lordly voice ordered the chauffeur to drive to the castle.

"I'm hungry," the fox said when they stopped in front of the castle made out of pure gold and silver, and he stepped out of the car.

"Yes indeed," responded a butler dressed in pure silk, and he motioned to twenty-four servants who carried glistening platters with meat, cheese, bread, fruit, butter, honey, chocolate, wine, raspberry juice, cigars, cigarettes, and candy. The fox ate, drank, smoked a cigar, and lay down to sleep in a bed of silk and velvet.

After sleeping two days, the fox awoke and said, "I'm warm."

"Yes indeed," responded the butler dressed in pure silk. He motioned to twelve of the servants, who brought the fox ice cream and iced coffee while the other twelve servants fanned the fox with palm leaves.

"I'm cold," said the fox after he had filled his stomach with the ice cream and iced coffee.

"Yes indeed, my lord," responded the butler dressed in pure silk. He motioned to the servants, who brought twenty-four pieces of fur. To the great astonishment of the fox, he found the fur of the wolf and the bear among them. My God, the fox thought to himself, if the strong wolf and the strong bear were treated as miserably as dogs, then it's probably a good idea for me to clear out of here.

The fox became as white as a sheet from fright, but he took enough time to grab some more cigars from a box and to drink a glass of champagne. Then he quickly took the fur pieces of the wolf and the bear, placed them under his arm, and jumped sprightfully out of the window.

"My lord, my lord!" the butler shouted after the fox, but he could shout as long as he might; the fox would not return. Indeed, he ran so fast that he did not even have time to smoke his cigar to an end by the time he reached the middle of the forest. After he listened to make sure he hadn't been followed, he entered the little cottage.

"I'm here again," he said and puffed some gigantic rings of smoke while the wolf and the bear wept tears of joy.

Now that the fox knew he was safe again, he greatly regretted that he had left the castle so hastily. That is why he stuck out his chest and showed off by smoking another cigar and blowing huge rings of smoke with all of his might.

"Well, friends, you certainly had your share of troubles." The fox laughed.

"We're just fortunate that you brought back our furs to us," the wolf said.

"I've done it this time, but it cost me a great deal to get your furs. And that's why I'll give them back to you only if you promise me that you won't do a thing without consulting me from now on," the fox explained. "I'll tell you both what you're to do, and I want you to follow all my orders."

The wolf and the bear looked at each other.

"He's talking just like the green man," said the wolf.

"He's talking just like the blue man," the bear said.

"What did you do while you were among the humans?" the wolf asked the fox.

"I was a lord," the fox responded proudly. "What did you do?"

"We were poor workers."

"What jackasses you were!" the fox laughed, but his laughter didn't last long because the bear smacked him so hard in the face that his cigar went flying, and the wolf pounded his chest so hard that the fox could only see countless green and blue circles dancing before his eyes.

"You're not jackasses, you're not jackasses!" exclaimed the fox. "Those human beings who served me are jackasses because they gave me so many good things without my having to work for them. And they're jackasses for working the way they did, for just being satisfied with the crumbs that fell from my table!"

Freedom through Solidarity

Heinrich Schulz

The Quiet Engine Room
(1924)

he engine blinked its eyes sleepily in the room, for it thought it heard a noise just then. Was it possible that the workers had returned? Nobody could be seen, but there it was again, the noise.

Buzz—buzzzz—boom-boom—buzz—boom! What was it?

Ah, a bee, a plain, ordinary bee had flown through a broken window into the engine room, and it couldn't find its way back out into the open. The bee became excited and clumsily tried to use its thick head to break through the hard window time and again.

Buzzzz —buzzzz —boom-boom —buzz —buzz — boom!

The engine closed its eyes again and continued to dream.

God, how sensitive it had become! A fly could now wake it from its sleep! If someone had told the engine four weeks ago how sensitive it would become, it would have laughed! The engine had always been so tired when the factory whistle blew to end the day that it would almost fall asleep before the workers had left the room.

Buzz—boom-boom-boom—buzz—buzz—buzz!

Again it heard the bee bump against the window, and it was getting annoyed that such a little twirp could prevent it from sleeping. It blinked toward the window and saw how the bee kept moving farther away from the hole through which it had first come.

"You there, little bee!" the engine shouted. "Where do you want to go?"

"Out, I want to get out of this cursed cage!"

"Hey, now, what do you mean by calling our room a cage? Are we prisoners?"

"What are you then? You're stuck here, and if the workers don't come and switch you on, you've got to remain quiet and stand still like blobs."

"That's true enough, but when we begin to operate, we perform useful work while you're nothing but a lazy tramp."

Buzzz —buzzz —boom —buzz —boom-boom —buzzzz!

"You don't like to hear the truth, do you, my little bee?"

"Oh, let me alone with your talk! Just tell me how to get out of here!"

"First, tell me what you're doing here. Are you a strikebreaker?"

"A strikebreaker? Phooey! Do I look like a strike-breaker?"

"Not exactly. I was just asking."

"But I did get lost in here because of the strike."

"Because of the strike? Listen, my friend, this inter-ests me. And the others, too. You see, they've all wak-ened up now. The forge, the anvil, the stamping ma-chine, the driving belts. We haven't heard or seen a thing about the strike for over four weeks."

"Did you hear anything about it before that?"

"Naturally. The workers talked about it. And then on the last day, when they all stopped working and looked at us for a long time, some of them certainly asked them-selves whether they would ever see us again."

"And since then you haven't heard a thing?"

"No, since then nobody's been here. We all think that the strike must still be going on because the workers haven't returned. But tell us what's going on, little bee. I didn't mean to insult you before."

"You called me a tramp. Well, it's exactly because I tramp around that I know what's happening every-where."

"Like what?"

"Like here!"

"What do you mean, here? I don't understand."

"What's going on here?"

"Nothing."

"You see. Well, nothing's going on outside either."

"Aha, now I understand, little bee. Nobody's working anywhere. It's just like here."

"That's the way it is. The chimneys have stopped puffing smoke. The machines have stopped working. Just a few trains travel back and forth, and in the harbor the ships just lie next to one another, and there are no workers to unload their freight. It's the same everywhere. The workers won't lift a hand, and it's so quiet and still that it's like Sunday all the time."

"That makes us all very happy. You see, we're for the workers!"

"It's only right. I'm also for the workers."

"That's nice of you, little bee!"

"Don't mention it! Incidentally, it's something to be taken for granted if you yourself don't have much money. Those workers are really remarkable men! They're not afraid to starve as though it were part of their job. And even the children are doing their share without grumbling."

"The children! I feel sorry for them. The machinist who operates me has a ten-year-old boy who always brought him food. I wish I could see him again!"

"You'll probably have to wait for some time. It was your very own machinist who told his wife last night that it will take ten horses to drag him into the factory again if they don't settle the strike in a fair way."

"That makes me happy! That's just like him! And I'm sure that he misses me just as much as I miss him. Were you at his home?"

"Yes, last night. And he also told his wife that he had the uneasy feeling that something might be wrong in the factory. He feared that strikebreakers might be operating his engine and had dirtied and perhaps ruined it, his beautiful, clean engine!"

"He said that? You mean, he thinks about me?"

"Of course. And then I took it upon myself to fly here today and check everything out. And if everything is all right, I want to buzz it into his ear while he's dreaming."

"My God, little bee, you really are nice. Who would have thought this, especially after you woke us all up with your buzzing!"

"That's the way it is sometimes. You can't always tell a book by its cover. Tell me, how do I get out of here?"

"Fly a little lower, a little more, just a bit more—that's it—and now fly a little more to the left—straight ahead over the frame—"

Buzzz—buzzzz—buzzzz—.

Dusk lowered its veil gradually over the factory.

And it became quiet again where hammers used to boom and engines used to roar.

It became very quiet.

Hermynia Zur Mühlen

The Glasses
(1923)

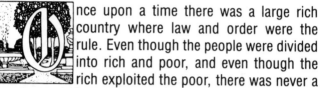nce upon a time there was a large rich country where law and order were the rule. Even though the people were divided into rich and poor, and even though the rich exploited the poor, there was never a word of complaint to be heard, much less gripes and threats. The king sat on his throne, fat, flabby, and content. The wealthy citizens were fat, flabby, and content in their beautiful homes. And the poor people worked diligently twelve hours a day in the fields and factories, and if they did not get enough to eat or did not earn enough, they appeared not to notice it.

There was a good reason for that. Hundreds of years ago an evil man who was the king's friend lived in this land. The magician could look into the future, and he realized that the poor people would not let themselves be treated like animals forever. One day they would demand their rights, and then the glory of the kings and wealthy citizens would end. And he wanted to prevent that. So, for the remainder of his life, the magician sat in his laboratory, where he cut glass into small round pieces. He tinged the glass with different colors and made them into eyeglasses. Then he told the king that he and his heirs were to order all newborn babies to wear glasses immediately after birth or else they would be sentenced to death.

Numerous glasses were stored in an enormous room, wrapped in special protective covers. An ancestor of the magician was placed in charge there, and he was informed each time a child was born. He then selected the appropriate glasses and even placed them on the little

Hermynia Zur Mühlen, *Ali, der Teppichweber* (Berlin: Malik, 1923). Illustrator: John Heartfeld. Cover art.

nose of the child, or he had one of his underlings take care of it.

There were different kinds of glasses. The most complicated were those the children of the poor people had to wear. The old magician had to work nearly fifty years before he could make them exactly right. The glasses were cut in such a way that the poor people who wore them saw their brothers and sisters as small, helpless, inferior creatures. However, if they looked at the wealthy citizens and at the king, such people seemed to be magnified as powerful, clearly godlike creatures who deserved all of the best things in the world—people whose power was irresistible and who had the right to make all other people into their servants. The old magician had found it extremely difficult to invent the right color for these glasses because they had to give their wearers the impression that their miserable homes were very comfortable and beautiful whenever they looked at their dwellings. On the other hand, the glasses also had to prevent them from recognizing the splendor and glory of the wealthy people's mansions and gardens or the king's castles and parks when they passed by; otherwise the poor people would ultimately become discontent.

It had been easier for the magician to make the glasses for the wealthy citizens. Here he merely mixed a little gold or silver with the glass so that the citizens always saw gold and silver but never living creatures, no matter where they looked. These glasses were cut in such a way that the workers seemed to be machines for the exclusive use of the wealthy citizens.

The glasses for the king gave the magician no trouble at all. They did not even have to be cut. He just dipped them once in the blood of the cruelest person who had ever lived and twice in the blood of the dumbest person who had ever lived. When the king wore the glasses, he saw whatever kings are accustomed to seeing, and he saw it in the way that suited all kings.

There was also a small number of large, rose-colored

glasses, which were very rarely used. In the three centuries since the death of the old magician, his descendants had had to use them only three times. These glasses had been made for those strange people whose eyes saw something of reality in spite of the customary glasses.

For instance, there was once a young poet who led a splendid life in the castle, and as court poet he was full of joy. All of the citizens respected and honored him. He wrote beautiful poems in praise of the king and his wise government, and he also wrote cheerful songs for the citizens and praised their virtues. One would have thought that the young poet was the happiest man in the world, and in fact, he did see only the bright side of the world through his silver glasses. Of course, despite all of their respect for the young poet, the citizens were somewhat disturbed that he had not become as soft and flabby as they were. However, because he was a poet, they forgave him.

One day the poet lost his way in the poor district of the city. It was a glorious summer day, and the sun was so hot that the silver of his glasses melted. With one eye the poet saw reality, and it horrified him so much that he gave forth a great cry. He saw tired, hardworking men, haggard, sick women, and shriveled, starving children. It seemed to him that he was the only person to have seen this until then, and he had to make it all known. He ran to the citizens, crying and burying his head in his hands, all the while telling them about the terrible things he had seen. They laughed and thought that the heat had made him somewhat crazy. Then he looked up at them, and his one eye saw the reality. He yelled at the citizens: "Robbers! Murderers!" and he raced to the king, for he hoped to find help there. However, when he glimpsed the king sitting on his throne, he was forced to shout, "You wicked, cruel fool! What right do you have to sit on the throne?"

The king had the poet put in chains and carried away.

The young man would certainly have been executed if the magician, the keeper of the glasses, had not put in a good word for him and explained to the king how the damage had been done. So the raving poet was dragged to the magician, who placed some rose-colored glasses on his nose and said, "Your old glasses were spoiled, my friend. That's why you thought you saw horrible things. Go now onto the streets, look around you, and you will realize your mistake."

The poet obeyed, and now everything seemed to be good and beautiful through his rose-colored glasses. Poverty appeared to be something holy and splendid, and he thought to himself: Work ennobles the people and makes them honorable—how lucky are those who are free to work and ennoble themselves twelve hours a day. Once again he recognized the citizens as virtuous friends, and when he reappeared before the king, he was dazzled by his majesty's splendor, and he sank to his knees in awe.

After that incident there were many, many years of law and order again. However, when the young poet became an old poet and lay on his deathbed, he brushed the glasses from his weak eyes, and for a brief moment he believed he saw again what he had seen on that summer day. A young maid nursed him with care and sat by his bedside. The poet grasped her hand and stammered, "The glasses, take them off and see!"

Then he died.

The young maid went home and thought about what the poet had said, and she was somewhat confused. To be sure, she had not understood the words of the dying man because the glasses not only influenced the eyes but also the minds of those who wore them. However, she always remembered the words of the poet and sometimes asked herself in secret how the world might look if she were to take off her glasses.

Soon thereafter she married a shoemaker, and when their first child was born, a splendid little boy, she saw his shining eyes and recalled the words of the poet. Then she felt it a shame that those beautiful eyes had to be hidden behind some ugly glasses. Still, there was nothing one could do. The magician came, placed some glasses on little Fritz's nose, and thus, everything was in order.

However, something strange happened. Little Fritz could not stand the glasses and tried time and again to take them off, so the parents lived in constant fear that he might succeed one time. He might run into the streets without his glasses, be caught by the guardians of order, and executed by the laws of the land. All of their pleas and threats amounted to nothing. As soon as Fritz was alone, he tore and yanked at the repulsive glasses that were tied to the back of his head in an ingenious manner.

As the boy grew up, he succeeded at times in tearing off the glasses, and his horrified eyes saw terrible things: on the one hand, there was misery and need and helplessness; on the other, there was wealth, comfort, splendor, and injustice. However, he caught only a glimpse of this because his mother or sister would always come running after him when he took off his glasses. They scolded, pleaded, and cried until he put his glasses on again.

Still the little he saw was enough to arouse great sadness and anger in the growing boy. He constantly thought of ways to rid the world of the injustice he perceived, and finally he became convinced that the glasses were responsible for everything. If his friends and comrades were to look at the world without glasses, they would realize that they were being wronged, and they would also see that they were not at all so weak and helpless as their glasses made it seem.

So one day, while his father was working in the shop and his mother and sister were in the kitchen, Fritz tore off his glasses, threw them on the ground, and trampled them into a thousand pieces. At first his newborn eyes were numbed by what they saw, as if he had been stunned by a blow to his head. However, soon a fire began to flare up in his heart and completely consumed him. He swore not to relax or rest until his friends had taken off their glasses, too, and really began to see.

But first it was important to conceal his deed from the citizens and the king. So Fritz tied a black cloth around his eyes and explained that the light hurt them. The citizens were satisfied with this explanation because they believed that it was more difficult to see through a black cloth than through the glasses.

When the darkness of the night protected him, Fritz sneaked outside and visited his friends. He told them what he saw and encouraged them to throw away their glasses. At first they laughed at him. But after he was able to convince a few of them to take off their glasses for a brief time, they took his side. As the days passed, there were more and more who took off their glasses until three fourths of the workers finally belonged to the "enemies of the glasses."

One day the "enemies of the glasses" armed themselves and were ready to give their all. They marched forth and invaded the houses of the wealthy citizens and demanded their rights from the king in his palace. His Majesty became so horrified that he rushed into the street and began to run. He ran and ran until he came to a country where the people still wore glasses and where law and order prevailed. Back in his kingdom, the wealthy citizens resisted at first; but once their glasses were torn from them, they recognized that the power of the "enemies of the glasses" was strong, and they realized that they themselves were wretched, dumb, and wicked. They grumbled, and their hearts were filled with anger as they were forced to obey the commands of the "enemies of the glasses."

However, there was a real and new order in the country now. Whoever worked earned enough money to live very well. Whoever loafed received nothing. The children and the old and sick people were all tended carefully, and nobody received more than his due.

The country where all this took place is in the East, where the sun rises. Perhaps the sun is brighter there, and the people have learned to see more quickly than the people in other countries. Yet we all know how fast light can travel, and it will travel to the other countries, and the people will break their glasses. Once they have really learned to *see*, then they will act accordingly. In the countries where darkness reigns each person must still do his part. Everyone must rip off the glasses, break them, and tell the others what he has seen, and he must recruit "enemies of the glasses" until their number is so large that they can become masters of a happy and free world.

Notes on Authors

Béla Balázs

(pseudonym for Herbert Bauer, 1884–1949)

Balázs, whose parents were teachers, was born in Szeged, Hungary. He was an excellent student and received a Ph.D. from the University of Budapest in 1909. He participated in World War I as a common soldier, and his experiences with the autocracy of the military politicized him. At the end of the war he joined the Hungarian Communist party and became one of the leaders of the Hungarian revolutionary movement. In 1920 he had to flee Hungary when the *Räterepublik* (soviet republic) collapsed. He eventually settled in Berlin, where he was active as a film director, theorist, and journalist. In 1924 he published a book on film entitled *Der sichtbare Mensch* (The Visible Man), which is still considered a major book in cinematic studies.

His interest in fairy tales began during his student years in Hungary, and he was particularly drawn to Oriental and Hungarian folktales. In 1917 he published his first collection of political fairy tales, entitled *Seven Fairy Tales,* and during the 1920s he continued adapting traditional folktales and writing original fairy tales for children that mirrored the political problems in Central Europe. Most of these works appeared in German: *Der Mantel der Träume* (The Cloak of Dreams, 1922) and *Das richtige Himmelblau* (The Right Kind of Blue Skies, 1925). By far his most significant work for children was the play *Hans Urian geht nach Brod* (Hans Urian Goes in Search of Bread, 1929), which he wrote with Lisa Tetzner. This fairy-tale drama about a young boy's magical learning experiences during the Depression was a great success in Germany and was later published as a fairy-tale novel. In 1931 Balázs emigrated to the Soviet Union and worked in various film studios. During this time he wrote antifascist novels for children: *Karlchen, durchhalten!* (Little Carl, Don't Give up! 1936) and *Heinrich beginnt den Kampf* (Henry Begins the Battle, 1941). At the close of World War II he returned to Budapest and headed the Institute for the Study of Film until his death in 1949.

"The Victor" was published as "Der Sieger" in Marguerite E. Benz, ed., *Für unsere kleinen russischen Brüder: Gaben westeuropäischer Schriftsteller und Künstler für die Notleidenden Kinder in den Hungerdistrikten Rußlands* (Geneva: 1922).

Carl Ewald

(1856–1908)

Ewald grew up in Bredelykke ved Gram, a small Danish city that was under German rule in the 1850s and 1860s. His father, H. F. Ewald, was a well-known novelist and Danish nationalist. He moved his family to Elsinore, Denmark, in 1864 because he could not tolerate being governed by the Germans. A stern and didactic disciplinarian, he sent his son Carl to high school in nearby Fredricksborg and hoped he would pursue a respectable career. Once Carl received his diploma, he decided to study forestry; however, he suffered a severe malady in 1874 that prevented him from becoming a forester, and he began teaching and writing, bent on breaking away from his father's conservative influence.

In 1880 Ewald moved to Copenhagen and earned his living as a journalist and free-lance writer. Soon he made a name for himself with a series of novels such as *The Rule or the Exception* (1883), *A Way Out* (1884), and *The Linden Branch* (1886), all of which exposed hypocrisy and corruption in Danish society. Strongly influenced by social Darwinism, Ewald depicted the brutal struggles for survival as a result of natural and social forces that shaped humankind's destiny. During the 1880s he effectively incorporated his social Darwinist principles into three important collections of fairy tales: *In the Open* (*I det Fri*, 1892), *Five New Fairy Tales* (*Fem nye Eventyr*, 1894), and *The Four Little Princes* (*Die fire Fjendingsfyrsten*, 1896). The public response was so favorable that he wrote another twenty volumes of fairy tales and also translated the fairy tales of the Brothers Grimm in 1905.

By the turn of the twentieth century Ewald became the most significant Danish fairy-tale writer in Germany, next to Hans Christian Andersen. However, in contrast to Andersen's optimistic perspective, Ewald was much more skeptical and cynical. His tales do not exude a "happy ending" ideology, and it was exactly because of their grim realism that they had a wide reception in Germany during the 1920s. His collected works were published there in five volumes: *Mutter Natur erzählt* (1910), *Der Zweifüßler und andere Geschichten* (1911), *Vier feine Freunde und andere Geschichten* (1913), *Meister Reineke und andere Geschichten* (1919), and *Das Sternekind und andere Geschichten* (1925). Not only were his tales popular in Germany, but they also made their way to England and the United States. For instance *Two-Legs and Other Stories* was published in 1907 and *The Old Willow-Tree and Other Stories* appeared in 1921.

"A Fairy Tale about God and the Kings" ("Ein Märchen von Gott und den Königen") was published in Ernst Friedrich, ed., *Proletar-*

ischer Kindergarten (Berlin: Buchverlag der Arbeiter-Kunstaus-stellung, 1921).

Felix Fechenbach

(1894–1933)

Fechenbach grew up in a baker's family and worked during his teens as an apprentice in a shoe store. In 1911 he joined the Social Democratic party (SPD) and immediately became active in the party's youth movement. Soon thereafter he was fired from a job he held in Frankfurt am Main because he led a strike against unpaid work. In 1912 he went to Munich, where he was employed in the SPD central office for workers. During World War I he was a pacifist, and after the war he played a major role in the Munich Räterepublik (soviet republic) as personal secretary to Kurt Eisner, the prime minister. When the Republic was invaded and dissolved by federal troops in the spring of 1919, he was arrested and sentenced to eleven years imprisonment. However, he was pardoned in 1924 and went to Berlin, where he began working with the organization Kinderfreunde (Friends of Children). As a result of this work he wrote and published Punch and Judy plays, fables, and children's songs that reflect his criticism of the SPD's politics during the Weimar Republic, though he remained a member of the party. Typical of his critical perspective are his fables, which depict the cowardly regressive politics of Social Democrats who betray their revolutionary instincts.

In 1929 Fechenbach became editor of the SPD's *Detmolder Parteiblatt,* and when the Nazis came to power in 1933, he was arrested because of his antifascist activities. Shortly thereafter, as he was being transported to the Dachau concentration camp, he was murdered by Nazi guards. Most of his fables had been published in newspapers and were reissued in Swiss exile by his friend Walter Victor in a book entitled *Die Lebensgemeinschaft: Das Felix-Fechenbach-Buch* (1936).

"The Chameleon" ("Der Chamäleon"), "The Triumph of the Wolves" ("Der Triumph der Wölfe"), and "The Revolution in the Zoo" ("Die Revolution im Zoo") were published in Walter Victor, ed., *Das Felix Fechenbach-Buch* (Zurich: Eichenverlag, 1936).

Oskar Maria Graf

(1894–1967)

Graf was born in Starnberg and was strongly influenced by Bavarian village life. He grew up in a hardworking family—his parents were bakers—and he left home at seventeen after many disputes with his older brother. In Munich, which became his new home, he worked as a miller, postman, and elevator boy while mixing in Bohemian circles. Like many other German writers of his time Graf was politicized by World War I. He participated in the November Revolution in 1918 and was a supporter of the Munich Räterepublik (soviet republic). During the 1920s he wrote novels, stories, essays, and autobiographical works that dealt with the provinciality of Bavarian village life and the social conditions that led to the downfall of the Weimar Republic. In 1927 he published a collection of fairy tales for children, *Licht und Schatten* (Light and Shadow) that made use of traditional folklore to shed light on various facets of authoritarianism that could be related to contemporary life in Germany. In particular, his tales focus on the brutality of tyrannical leaders who can be tamed only by supernatural forces more powerful than they are.

Because of his strong opposition to Nazism, he emigrated to Vienna in 1933, where he continued to write novels about the constraints of living in German villages and small towns. In addition, he became active in the antifascist resistance movement; but in 1938, with the annexation of Austria, he was forced to flee. He made his way to New York, where he spent the rest of his life. Just as he had done in his Austrian exile, Graf kept producing significant political works. Among his best were the two autobiographical volumes, *Menschen aus meiner Jugend auf dem Dorf* (People from my Youth in the Village, 1953) and *Gelächter von außen: Aus meinem Leben 1918–1933* (Laughter from Outside: About My Life 1918–1933, 1966), and a novel about exile life in New York, *Die Flucht ins Mittelmäßige* (The Flight into Mediocrity, 1966).

"The Fairy Tale about the King" ("Das Märchen vom König") and "Baberlababb" were published in *Licht und Schatten: Eine Sammlung zeitgemäßer Märchen* (Berlin: Verlag der Neuen Gesellschaft, 1927).

Robert Grötzsch

(1882–1946)

After learning the trade of plumbing, and traveling from job to job during his youth, Grötzsch eventually turned to writing by the turn of the century to earn his living. He had a fair amount of success by publishing satires, dramas, and children's books, and he also became a journalist for the SPD newspaper *Die Sächsische Arbeiter-Zeitung* in Dresden. His fairy-tale books, *Nauckes Luftreise* (1908),

Verschrobenes Volk (1912), *Muz der Riese* (1913), and *Der Zauberer Burufu* (1922), were popular with a general reading public and were actually reprinted a few times. Grötzsch employed comedy to depict the foibles of monstrous characters and expounded a deep faith in the potential of the common people to overcome despotism.

From 1919 to 1933 Grötzsch was editor-in-chief of the *Dresdner Volkszeitung,* but he was compelled to emigrate to Prague when the Nazis came to power because of his antifascist activities. Although he was able to resume his journalism career there, he had to flee the Nazis again when they occupied Czechoslovakia. He made his way first to Paris and then, in 1941, to New York, where he worked for various antifascist organizations and magazines until his death in 1946.

"The Magician Burufu" ("Der Zauberer Burufu"), "Felix the Fish" ("Felix der Fisch"), and "The Enchanted King" ("Der verzauberte König"), were published in *Der Zauberer Burufu* (Berlin: Dietz, 1922).

Edwin Hoernle

(1883–1952)

Hoernle spent his youth in the East Indies, where his father was a missionary. When he was a teenager, the family returned to Germany, and he attended high school in Ludwigsburg and Stuttgart. Following in his father's footsteps, he then studied theology and became a vicar in 1909. However, after three months he abandoned his faith in Christianity and moved to Berlin, where he made the acquaintance of Clara Zetkin, Franz Mehring, and Rosa Luxemburg, all leaders of the left wing of the Social Democratic party, which he joined in 1910. Hoernle did journalistic work for the SPD and edited the children's section of the women's Socialist newspaper, *Gleichheit.* When World War I erupted, Hoernle opposed military action, but he was arrested and forced to serve in the German army. During the war he was wounded at the front. In 1918 he helped form the Communist party and became one of the prominent leaders in the revolutionary educational movement. In 1920 he published *Die Occuli-Fabeln,* an anthology of radical fables and fairy tales, written during the war, which stress the necessity for revolutionary action. In particular, Hoernle criticized the Social Democratic party for compromising the goals of Socialists and Communists alike and undermining the power of the working classes. At the beginning of the 1920s he wrote numerous articles about progressive education, and in 1924 he became the leader of the Communist children's groups and the editor of the magazines *Der junge Genosse* and *Das prole-*

tarische Kind. Most of his essays on radical education were published in the book *Grundfragen der proletarischen Erziehung* (Basic Questions about Proletarian Education, 1929), which contained a key theoretical piece about radical fairy tales and the need to "proletarianize" the traditional fairy tale.

When the Nazis seized power in 1933, Hoernle made his way to the Soviet Union, where he worked in the International Agriculture Institute. After World War II he returned to East Germany and became the head of the ministry for agriculture and forestry and played a key role in reforming the farm system in the German Democratic Republic. He never resumed his work with young children, and his tales have received only scant attention in East Germany.

"The Giant and His Suit of Armor" ("Der Riese und seine Rüstung"), "The Little King and the Sun" ("Der kleine König und die Sonne"), "The Poodle and the Schnauzer" ("Der Pudel und der Schnauzer"), and "The Chameleon" ("Der Chamäleon") were published in *Die Occuli-Fabeln* (Stuttgart: Wöhrle, 1920).

Béla Illés

(1895–1974)

After fighting as a soldier during World War I, Illés became a pacifist and joined the Communist party in Hungary. Upon the collapse of the Hungarian *Räterepublik* (soviet republic) in 1920, he emigrated to Vienna and later settled in the Soviet Union, where he became a leading member of the International Organization of Revolutionary Writers. Many of his novels and stories were published in German for the German-speaking ethnic groups in the Soviet Union, and in 1925 his collection *Rote Märchen* (Red Fairy Tales) was issued by Freidenker Verlag in Leipzig. Illés made use of traditional oral tales and fables and expressionist techniques to draw parallels with political conditions in Europe. His major purpose was to illustrate in symbolic form lessons that the oppressed classes had to learn if they were to come out on top in the class struggle.

Illés remained in the Soviet Union throughout the 1930s, and during World War II he fought against the Germans as an officer in the Red Army. At the conclusion of the war he returned to Budapest, where he resumed his career as a writer and established a reputation as one of the finest prose stylists in Hungary.

"The Fairy Tale about the Bear, the Wolf and the Sly Fox" ("Das Märchen vom Bären, vom Wolf und vom schlauen Fuchs") was published in *Rote Märchen* (Leipzig: Freidenker Verlag, 1925).

Berta Lask

(1878–1967)

Born in Poland, Lask grew up in Pomerania, and as the daughter of a wealthy factory owner, she was able to take advantage of an excellent education that was to prove beneficial to her when she decided to become a writer later in her life. After her marriage as a young woman to a doctor L. Jacobsohn, she settled in Berlin, where her husband had his practice in a working-class district. As a result of her exposure to the poverty and social problems of the workers at the beginning of the twentieth century, she began writing poems and plays that reflected her concern for their plight. During World War I she joined the pacifist movement, and after the war she became a member of a radical anarchist group. However, by 1923 she realized that she would have to work within a major political party if she wanted to be effective, so she became a member of the Communist party.

A gifted writer, she worked closely with agit-prop groups, writing revolutionary dramas and skits such as *Thomas Münzer* (1925), *Leuna* (1927), and *Giftgasnebel über Sowjetrußland* (Poisonous Clouds of Gas over the Soviet Union, 1927). In addition to various fairy tales that she wrote in her early expressionist phase, Lask produced songs and poems for children, along with two books: *Auf dem Flügelpferde durch die Zeiten* (On the Flying Horse through Time, 1925) and *Wie Franz und Grete nach Rußland reisten* (How Franz and Greta Traveled to Russia, 1926). In 1929 she helped found the League of Proletarian-Revolutionary Writers, and in 1933 she was arrested by the Nazis, who killed her son. She was fortunate enough to be released after six months in prison, and she immediately emigrated to the Soviet Union, where she wrote political works for various magazines and for radio. In 1953 she returned to the German Democratic Republic and completed a book of antifascist stories for children, entitled *Otto und Else* (1956), and wrote an important novel trilogy entitled *Stille und Sturm* (Silence and Storm, 1955), which dealt largely with the remarkable events of her own life. Until her death in 1967, she played an active role in East German cultural affairs.

"The Boy Who Wanted to Fight with a Dragon" ("Die Geschichte vom dem Jungen, der mit einem Drachen kämpfen wollte") was published in Ernst Friedrich, ed., *Proletarischer Kindergarten. Ein Märchen- und Lesebuch für Kinder und Erwachsene* (Berlin: Buchverlag der Arbeiter-Kunstausstellung, 1921).

Eugen Lewin-Dorsch

(dates unknown)

There is no biographical data about Lewin-Dorsch available. He published "The Fairy Tale about the Wise Man" ("Das Märchen vom weisen Mann") in *Die Dollarmännchen* (Berlin: Malik, 1923). This book contains nine radical political fairy tales, which were illustrated by Heinrich M. Davringhausen.

Anna Mosegaard

(dates unknown)

In the early part of the 20th century Mosegaard was working in a factory when she began writing articles and stories for Social Democratic newspapers and magazines. From 1910 on she also produced one-act skits and farces for workers' theaters. During the Weimar Republic period she published more than twenty fairy-tale and Christmas plays for children in Leipzig, along with folk plays and comedies for adults. The general tendency of her work was to adapt traditional folk material in a manner that made it easy for children to grasp the comments about negative social conditions. For instance, in "The Giant Spider" she uses the popular legend about Rübezahl, a well-known mountain spirit in German folklore, to illustrate how greed and wealth can destroy the essence of a human being.

"The Giant Spider" ("Die Riesenspinne") appeared in *Kinderland* (1928), an annual magazine for children, and it is the only prose fairy tale that Mosegaard wrote for young readers.

Joachim Ringelnatz

(Hans Bötticher, 1883–1934)

Ringelnatz was the son of the well-known writer of children's books, Georg Bötticher, who also edited the important journal *Auerbachs Kinder-Kalendar*. He began writing tales for children as a young boy and published them in various anthologies and magazines. By the time Ringelnatz graduated from high school in 1901, however, he decided that he would rather travel than pursue a career as writer. So, with his parents' permission, he became a sailor on a ship that traveled to the West Indies. Thereafter, he had various occupations as salesman, book dealer, librarian, and actor. In 1909 he performed in Simplicissimus, the famous cabaret in Munich, and he began writing skits, poems, and stories for children. During World War I he served in the merchant marine, and after 1919 he resumed his career as cabaret artist and began writing for children again, achieving notoriety for his highly satirical skits and stories. Among his best-known books for children are *Kuttel Daddeldu erzählt seinen Kindern das Märchen vom Rotkäppchen* (1923), *Geheimes Kinder-Spiel-Buch* (1924), and *Das Kinder-Verwirr-Buch* (1931). Ringelnatz owed a great deal to the tradition of nonsense stories and rhymes. Highly experimental and innovative, he sought to turn traditional tales and conventions upside down to question social propriety and conformism. Because of the political criticism in his tales and witty skits, his cabaret performances were banned by the Nazis in 1933. One year later he died of tuberculosis in Berlin.

"Kuttel Daddeldu Tells His Children the Fairy Tale about Little Red Cap" ("Kuttel Dadeldu erzählt seinen Kindern das Märchen vom Rotkäppchen") was published in *Kuttel Daddeldu* (Munich: Kurt Wolff, 1923).

Bruno Schönlank

(1891–1965)

Born in Berlin, Schönlank was the son of the editor-in-chief of the SPD newspaper, the *Leipziger Volkszeitung*. After attending high school in Leipzig, he studied farming and worked as a farmer on a large estate in East Prussia for one year. Then he had a succession of jobs in factories and in a bookstore before traveling through different western European countries. When World War I began, he returned to Germany to help organize a peace demonstration, for which he was arrested. Shortly thereafter he was drafted into the German army but did not abandon his opposition to the war, and when the November Revolution of 1919 occurred in Berlin, Schönlank became active in the radical Spartakusbund and the Communist party.

In 1920, however, he left the KPD to join the Social Democratic party and wrote for various party newspapers and magazines. He became particularly well known for his chorus work with amateur groups in the workers movement. He also published two important collections of fairy tales, *Großstadt-Märchen* (Big-City Fairy Tales, 1923) and *Der Kraftbonbon und andere Großstadtmärchen* (The Power Candy and Other Big-City Fairy Tales, 1928), which incorporate magic to project the possibility for peaceful reconciliation of political conflicts. In that respect the happy endings of Schönlank's fairy tales were in accord with the SPD's general policies of compromising the class struggle.

Because of the active role he played within the SPD, as well as his antifascist stance, he was obliged to flee Germany as soon as the

Nazis came to power in 1933. He spent the rest of his life in Switzerland, where he continued to write stories and plays. In fact, Schönlank continued to experiment with fairy tales; among his later fairy-tale works are *Schweizer Märchen* (Swiss Fairy Tales, 1938) and *Doppelbukkelchen* (The Two Small Humps, 1965).

"The Patched Pants" ("Die geflickte Hose") was published in *Der Kraftbonbon und andere Großstadtmärchen* (Berlin: Büchergilde Gutenberg, 1928).

Heinrich Schulz

(1872–1932)

After studying at a school of education in Bremen, Schulz became a teacher but only for a short time. When he joined the Social Democratic party in 1893, he gave up teaching in the public school system as a career and became active in the SPD's educational office. In 1894 he moved to Berlin, where he helped direct the education school for workers and began writing articles about children's literature and education. From 1907 until 1920 Schulz was head of the SPD's political school in Berlin, and although he played an important role in elaborating Social Democratic policies, he argued against tendentious or overly didactic literature for children. Schulz sought to promote a "neutral" literature with high artistic quality that would stimulate the imagination of children and develop their ability to appreciate creative works.

In 1920, when the SPD came to power, Schulz became head of the cultural ministry and also began writing books for children. Among his publications are *Der kleine Jan* (1920), *Aus meinen vier Pfählen* (1921), *Jan Kiekindiewelt* (1924), and *Von Menschen, Tierlein und Dinglein: Märchen aus dem Alltag* (1924). This last book, a collection of fairy tales about daily life, was most important because the tales were conceived to clarify social relations and to offer possibilities for the solution of political conflicts. Schulz focused on the necessity to encourage solidarity among the workers and introduced proletarian elements into traditional folktales and fables. In this respect he remained true to his social democratic convictions until the end of his life.

"The Castle with the Three Windows" ("Das Schloß mit den drei Fenstern") and "The Quiet Engine Room" ("Der stille Maschinensaal") were published in *Von Menschlein, Tierlein und Dinglein* (Berlin: Dietz, 1924).

Kurt Schwitters

(1887–1948)

After a traditional education at art academies in Hannover, Dresden, and Berlin from 1909 to 1914, Schwitters served as a machine designer in the German army during World War I. By 1918, given the chaos of the times, he abandoned his imitational artwork and began to develop his special brand of dadaist art that used association and distortion to question "normal" standards and expectations of art audiences. He soon became known as one of the most experimental painters, sculptors, and poets in Germany and worked closely with such other innovative artists as Hans Arp, Theo von Doesburg, and Käte Steinitz. Aside from his painting and graphic work, Schwitters wrote unusual stories and fairy tales for children, such as *Der Hahnepeter* (1924), *Die Scheuche* (1925), and *Die Märchen vom Paradies* (1924), which incorporated original designs and print to stimulate the imagination of his readers. He called his unique method MERZkunst, fusing all kinds of aesthetic concepts and found objects in arrangements that challenged the traditional perspective of readers and viewers. The result in his fairy tales is parody, but they also offer new possibilities with regard to the autonomy of the reader. During the 1930s his art and writings were regarded as decadent by the Nazis, and in 1938 he emigrated to Norway. When the Nazis invaded Norway, he fled to England, where he spent the rest of his life painting traditional landscapes and portraits in order to support himself and his son.

"Happiness" ("Das Glück") was published in the *Hannoverscher Kurier,* November 25, 1925.

Maria Szucisch

(dates unknown)

In 1910 Szucisch settled in Budapest with her husband, Lajos Barta (1878–1964), who was considered the pioneer of socialist literature in Hungary. Szucisch had already written stories for children in various newspapers and magazines. During the Hungarian Räterepublik (soviet republic) in 1919 she edited a magazine for girls, and after her emigration to Germany in 1920 she published political fairy tales in various journals, along with two important books of her tales, *Die Träume des Zauberbuches* (The Dreams of the Magic Book, 1923) and *Silavus* (1924). Many of her fairy tales borrow motifs from traditional oriental tales, but she adapted them to address the social and political conflicts of her day. In particular,

Silavus is a series of fairy tales about the son of a mighty monarch who works against his father's despotic rule.

Because of the scant biographical information about Szucisch, it is unclear what happened to her once the Weimar Republic collapsed.

"The Holy Wetness" ("Von der heiligen Nässe") was published in *Silavus* (Berlin: Malik, 1924).

Hermynia Zur Mühlen

(1883–1951)

As the daughter of the wealthy Contessa Isabella Wydenbruck and the Count Victor Crenneville, Zur Mühlen traveled to many countries in Africa and Asia during her youth and was given a broad cosmopolitan education. In 1898 she was placed in a boarding school for girls in Dresden, and when she graduated in 1901, she wanted to become an elementary school teacher. However, her parents objected because they thought such a position was beneath her dignity as a member of the aristocratic class. Instead, Zur Mühlen was allowed to go to Geneva in 1903, where she learned the art of bookbinding and eventually came into contact with political emigrants who had left Russia during the upheavals in 1905. In 1907 she was compelled to marry a country gentleman named Count Zur Mühlen, who had estates on the Baltic Sea; the marriage was doomed to failure because she could not stand the patriarchal rules of aristocratic married life and the closed society in Russia. She was divorced in 1913, and when World War I erupted, she went to Switzerland because of a lung disease. It was there that Zur Mühlen made the acquaintance of the Hungarian writer and Communist, Stefan J. Klein, who became her lover and companion.

In 1919 they moved to Frankfurt am Main, where both made names for themselves as translators. Zur Mühlen translated such writers as Sinclair Lewis, Upton Sinclair, and Alexander Bogdanov, and Klein translated almost all of the important Hungarian writers of fairy tales such as Balázs, Illés, and Szucisch. Most important, Zur Mühlen herself became the leading writer of revolutionary fairy tales for children. Her major publications include *Was Peterchen Freunde erzählen* (What Little Peter's Friends Tell, 1920), *Märche* (Fairy Tales, 1922), *Ali, der Teppichweber* (Ali, The Carpet Weave 1923), *Das Schloß der Wahrheit* (The Castle of Truth, 1924), *Es wa einmal . . . und es wird sein* (Once Upon a Time . . . and It Will B 1930), *Schmiede der Zukunft* (Smiths of the Future, 1933). Her tale dealt with a variety of themes ranging from war to the exploitatic of the working class, and she experimented with the parable, all gory, and oriental folktale. Because of her political activities, she was forced to leave Germany in 1933, and she moved first to Vienna and then to Prague. A remarkably prolific writer, Zur Mühlen translated about 150 works and wrote 30 stories, novels, and mysteries to earn her living, while keeping active in the antifascist movement. In 1938 she emigrated to England, where she spent the latter part of her life, and published several interesting autobiographical works.

"The Servant" ("Der Knecht") and "The Glasses" ("Die Brillen") were published in *Ali, der Teppichweber* (Berlin: Malik, 1923), and "The Fence" ("Der Zaun") was published in *Das Schloß der Wahrheit* (Berlin: Verlag der Jugendinternationale, 1924).

Bibliography

Literary Criticism and History

Brackert, Helmut, ed. *Und wenn sie nicht gestorben sind . . . Perspektiven auf das Märchen.* Frankfurt am Main: Suhrkamp, 1980.

Dolle, Bernd, Dieter Richter, and Jack Zipes, eds. *Es wird einmal . . . Soziale Märchen der Zwanziger Jahre.* Munich: Weismann, 1983.

Dolle-Weinkauff, Bernd. *Das Märchen in der proletarisch-revolutionären Kinder- und Jugendliteratur der Weimarer Republik 1918–1933.* Frankfurt am Main: dipa-Verlag, 1984.

Dreher, Ingmar. *Die deutsche proletarisch-revolutionäre Kinder- und Jugendliteratur zwischen 1918 und 1933.* Berlin: Kinderbuchverlag, 1975.

Eykmann, Christoph. "Das Märchen im Expressionismus." In *Denk- und Stilformen des Expressionismus,* 125–43. Munich: Fink, 1974.

Gay, Peter. *Weimar Culture: The Outsider as Insider.* New York: Harper and Row, 1968.

Geerken, Hartmut. "Zur Märchendichtung im 20. Jahrhundert." In *Märchen des Expressionismus,* edited by Hartmut Geerken, 11–32. Frankfurt am Main: Fischer, 1979.

Geiß, Manfred. "Sozialistischer Kinder- und Jugendliteratur." In *Lexikon der Kinder- und Jugendliteratur,* edited by Klaus Doderer, vol. 3, 414–23. Weinheim: Beltz, 1979.

Hoernle, Edwin. *Grundfragen proletarischer Erziehung.* Edited by Lutz von Werder and Reinhart Wolff. 1929. Reprint. Darmstadt: März, 1969.

Hopster, Norbert, and Ulrich Nassen. *Märchen und Mühsal: Arbeit und Arbeitswelt in Kinder- und Jugendbüchern aus drei Jahrhunderten.* Bielefeld: Granier, 1988.

Kaiser, Bruno. "Zur Geschichte des proletarischen deutschen Kinderbuchs." *Almanach für die Freunde des Kinderbuchs* (1959): 33–41.

Möbius, Hanno. "Revolutionäre Märchen der zwanziger Jahre." *Kürbiskern* 7 (1971): 267–70.

Schlenstedt, Silvia. "Tat vermähle sich den Traum. Revolutionäres und Evolutionäres im Utopischen expressionistischer Literatur." In *Revolution und Literatur: Zum Verhältnis von Erbe, Revolution und Literatur,* edited by Werner Mittenzwei and Reinhard Weisbach, 129–58. Leipzig, 1971.

Tismar, Jens. *Das deutsche Kunstmärchen des 20. Jahrhunderts.* Stuttgart: Metzler, 1981.

Trommler, Frank. *Sozialistische Literatur in Deutschland: Ein historischer Überblick.* Stuttgart: Kröner, 1976.

Werder, Lutz von. *Sozialistische Erziehung in Deutschland 1848–1973.* Frankfurt am Main: Fischer, 1974.

Wührl, Paul-Wolfgang. *Das deutsche Kunstmärchen: Geschichte, Botschaft und Erzählstruktur.* Heidelberg: Quelle & Meyer, 1984.

Zipes, Jack. *Fairy Tales and the Art of Subversion: The Classical Genre for Children and the Process of Civilization.* New York: Methuen, 1983.

Fairy Tales

Balázs, Béla. *Sieben Märchen.* Translated by Else Sephani. Munich: Rikola, 1921.

———. *Das richtige Himmelblau.* Munich: Drei-Masken-Verlag, 1925.

———. *Der Mantel der Träume: Chinesische Novellen.* Munich: Bischoff, 1922.

———. *Hans Urian geht nach Brod; Eine Kindermärchenkomödie von heute.* In collaboration with Lisa Tetzner. Freiburg/Breslau, 1929.

Bodanzki, Robert. "König Kapital: Ein Gegenwartsmärchen aus uralten Zeiten." In *Das freie Jugendbuch,* edited by Heinz Jacoby, 14–20. Berlin-Charlottenburg: Verlag Neues Ziel, 1927.

Eschbach, Walter. *Märchen der Wirklichkeit.* Leipzig: E. Oldenburg, 1924.

Ewald, Carl. *Ausgewählte Märchen.* Leipzig: Leipziger Buchdruckerei, 1918.

———. *Märchen.* Leipzig: Leipziger Buchdruckerei, 1919.

Fechenbach, Felix. *Das Felix-Fechenbach-Buch.* Edited by Walter Victor. Zurich: Eichenverlag, 1936.

Friedrich, Ernst, ed. *Proletarischer Kindergarten: Eine Märchen- und Lesebuch für Groß und Klein.* Berlin: Buchverlag der Arbeiter-Kunstausstellung, 1921.

Goes, Gustav. *Ins Märchenland.* Berlin: Klemm, 1922.

Graf, Georg Engelbert. *Die Geschichte von den Eisriesen: Ein Märchen aus der großen Schneezeit.* Jena: Thüringer Verlagsanstalt, 1923.

———. *Ein Märchen vom Rhein und von den Menschen.* Jena: Thüringer Verlagsanstalt, 1925.

———. *Riesen und Knirpse: Erdgeschichte in Märchen.* Jena: Urania-Freidenker-Verlag, 1931.

Graf, Oskar Maria. *Licht und Schatten: Eine Sammlung zeitgemäßer Märchen*. Berlin: Verlag der Neuen Gesellschaft, 1927.

Grötzsch, Robert. *Nauckes Luftreise und andere Wunderlichkeiten*. Dresden: Kaden, 1908.

———. *Muz, der Riese: Ein heiteres Abenteuermärchen*. 3rd ed. Dresden: Kaden, 1927.

———. *Der Zauberer Burufu*. Berlin: Dietz, 1922.

Hoernle, Edwin. *Die Oculi-Fabeln*. Stuttgart: Oskar Wöhrle, 1920.

Illés, Béla. *Rote Märchen*. Translated by Stefan J. Klein. Leipzig: Freidenker Verlag, 1924.

Jacoby, Heinz, ed. *Das freie Jugendbuch*. Berlin-Charlottenburg: Verlag Neues Ziel, 1927.

Keller, Paul. *Grünlein*. Breslau: Bergstadt Verlag, 1915.

Krüger, Hilde. *Der Wünschebold*. Berlin: Dietz, 1925.

Lask, Berta. "Die Geschichte von dem Jungen, der mit einem Drachen kämpfen wollte." In *Proletarischer Kindergarten,* edited by Ernst Friedrich, 19–23. Berlin: Buchverlag der Arbeiter-Kunst-Ausstellung, 1921.

———. *Auf dem Flügelpferde durch die Zeiten: Bilder vom Klassenkampf der Jahrtausende*. Berlin: Vereinigung Internationaler Verlagsanstalten, 1925.

———. *Wie Franz und Grete nach Rußland reisten*. Berlin: Vereinigung Internationaler Verlagsanstalten, 1926.

Lengyel, Jozsef. *Sternkund und Reinekund*. Translated by Stephan J. Klein. Dresden: Verlagsanstalt proletarischer Freidenker Deutschlands, 1923.

Lesebuch für Arbeiterkinder. Berlin: Verlag Junge Garde, 1926.

Lewin-Dorsch, Eugen. *Die Dollarmännchen*. Vol. 2 of *Märchen der Armen*. Berlin: Malik, 1923.

Liebersen, Maria. "Wie die Rotkehlchen den Zaren besiegten." In *Lesebuch für Arbeiterkinder*. Berlin: Verlag Junge Garde, 1926.

Meyer-Leviné, Rosa, trans. *Lenin-Märchen: Volksmärchen aus der Sowjetunion*. Roter Trommler, vol. 7. Berlin: Verlag der Jugendinternationale, 1929.

Mosegaard, Anna. "Die Riesenspinne." In *Kinderland* (Berlin: Vorwärts Buchdruckerei, 1928.

Ringelnatz, Joachim. *Kuttel Daddeldu*. Munich: Kurt Wolff, 1923.

———. *Geheimes Kinder-Spiel-Buch mit vielen Bildern*. Potsdam: Gustav Kiepenheuer, 1924.

———. *Kinder-Verwirr-Buch mit vielen Bildern*. Berlin: Ernst Rowohlt, 1931.

Rona, Irene. *Was Paulchen werden will*. Berlin: Vereinigung Internationaler Verlagsanstalten, 1926.

Schönlank, Bruno. *Großstadtmärchen*. Berlin: Verlag für Sozialwissenschaft, 1924.

————. *Der Kraftbonbon und andere Großstadtmärchen.* Berlin: Büchergilde Gutenberg, 1928.

Schulz, Heinrich. *Von Menschlein, Tierlein und Dinglein: Märchen aus dem Alltag.* Berlin: Dietz, 1924.

Schwitters, Kurt. *Die Märchen vom Paradies.* Hannover: Apossverlag, 1924.

————. *Die Schleuche.* Hannover, Apossverlag, 1925.

————. "Das Glück." *Hannoverscher Kurier,* November 25, 1925, 2.

Strzelewicz, Willi. *Die Revolution im Zwergenland: Märchenspiel mit Gesang und Tanz in einem Akt.* Leipzig: Arbeiter-Theaterverlag Alfred Jahn, 1924.

Swirski, Alexej I. *Schwarze Leute: Erzählungen aus dem Bergmannsleben.* Translated by Hermynia Zur Mühlen. Berlin: Verlag der Jugendinternationale, 1923.

Szucisch, Mária. *Die Träume des Zauberbuches.* Dresden: Verlagsanstalt proletarischer Freidenker Deutschlands, 1923.

————. *Silavus.* Translated by Stefan J. Klein. Vol. 4 of *Märchen der Armen.* Berlin: Malik, 1924.

Tetzner, Lisa. *Vom Märchenbaum der Welt.* Berlin: Büchergilde Gutenberg, 1929.

————. *Hans Urian: Die Geschichte einer Weltreise.* Berlin: Weiß, 1929.

Vaillant-Couturier, Paul. *Hans ohne Brot (Jean sans pain).* Translated by Anna Nussbaum. Berlin: Verlag der Jugendinternationale, 1928.

Weisbart, Josef. *Der Wunderquell und Rotnäschen.* Berlin: Deutscher Arbeiter-Abstinentenbund, 1925.

Wolf, Arthur, ed. *Pflug und Saat: Soziale Erzählungen, Fabeln, Skizzen und Gedichte.* Dresden: Verlagsanstalt für proletarische Freidenker, 1923.

Wolfgang, Otto. "Das Märchen vom Gott Mammon." *Heimstunden* 3 (1925): 193–204.

Zerfaß, Julius. *Die Reise mit dem Lumpensack.* Berlin: Dietz, 1925.

Zur Mühlen, Hermynia. *Was Peterchens Freunde erzählen.* Vol. 1 of *Märchen der Armen.* Berlin: Malik, 1921.

————. *Märchen.* Berlin: Vereinigung Internationaler Verlagsanstalten, 1922.

————. *Der kleine graue Hund.* Berlin: Vereinigung Internationaler Verlags-Anstalten, 1922.

————. *Ali, der Teppichweber.* Berlin: Malik, 1923.

————. *Das Schloß der Wahrheit.* Berlin: Verlag der Jugendinternationale, 1924.

————. *Der Muezzin.* Berlin: Verlag der Jugendinternationale, 1927.

————. *Said, der Träumer.* Roter Trommler, vol. 6. Berlin: Verlag der Jugendinternationale, 1927.

————. *Die Söhne der Aischa.* Roter Trommler, vol. 4. Berlin: Verlag der Jugendinternationale, 1927.

————. *Es war einmal . . . und es wird sein.* Berlin: Verlag der Jugendinternationale, 1930.

————. *Schmiede der Zukunft.* Berlin: Verlag der Jugendinternationale, 1933.